From the forgotten queens of sci-fi and horror pulps, to vignettes of Black life in Chicago in the late 1950s, to time-traveling and galaxy-hopping puns, our **Beyond Pulp Reprints** series brings neglected works back into print in editions that are both attractive and affordable.

THROUGH TIME AND SPACE WITH FERDINAND FEGHOOT

REGINALD BRETNOR

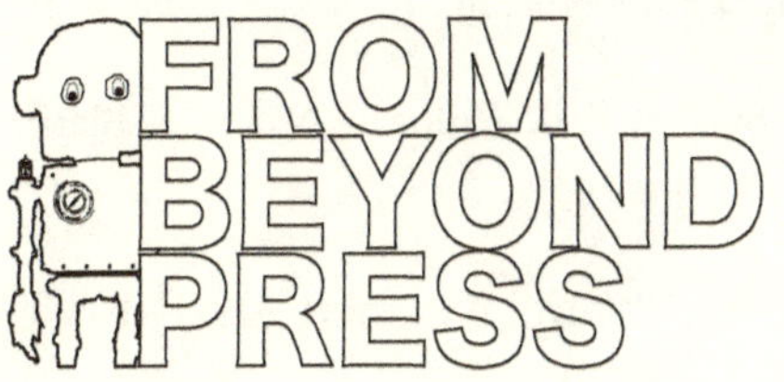

Library of Congress Control Number: 2024948928
ISBN: 979-8-9875743-7-9

)(

The Time-Travellers Club
7-10 King Charles III Street
London, S.W. 1

CONTENTS

) ILLUSTRATIONS (

DEAN SMITH

Sometime in 1991, in Eugene, Oregon, I was in my office at Pulphouse Publishing. I was the publisher, and we had a two-story office building that was more a beehive than anything else.

The place was super fun and super stressful.

I was very young it seemed, looking back from 40 years in the future, and I had no idea how lucky I was to have major writers like Algis Budrys, Robert Sheckly, and others just always stopping by when they came through town.

My wife, Kristine Kathryn Rusch, had just accepted the editorship at the *Magazine of Fantasy and Science Fiction (F&SF)*

I was also a fan of the history of the pulp magazines and a real fan of the history of *F&SF* from its start in 1949. In fact, Kris and I had (and still have) a full run of the magazine.

So I was sort of out of place in time and space when one of my employees knocked on my door and said, "There is a writer downstairs by the name of Reginald Bretnor to see you and Kris."

I have to admit that it took me a few beats to finally register the name. Reginald Bretnor, one of the great writers in modern science fiction, and the author of some of funniest fantasy and science fiction stories ever written.

Seems he lived in Medford about three hours south of us and mostly wanted to meet the new editor of *F&SF*. I quickly filled in Kris that Reg had published a story in *F&SF* in basically the first full year of the magazine and had been a regular contributor ever since.

And that he had written some of the humor classics in *F&SF*. (At that moment I did not know he also wrote all the Feghoots.)

I remember that afternoon, we had a wonderful chat in a nearby restaurant and we bought him lunch. I was a little bit (maybe more than a little) gosh-wowed by him at first, but he was so nice, so kind, so totally dapper in his suit, tie, polished shoes, and no hair out of place, he soon worked me past that. Actually it was his laugh that relaxed me the most.

And it was in that meal that I learned that Grendel Briarton, the author of the Feghoots, wonderful, funny short science fiction and fantasy stories, was also Reginald Bretnor.

Feghoots are almost all very short twist stories in the style of O. Henry, only with attitude, and starred a character by the name of Feghoot. Over time readers and writers of short, funny twist stories called their stories Feghoots, even though Reg owned the name.

Over the next year, Reg stopped by the office a number of times and Kris and I always looked forward to seeing him. At one point the three of us came up with the idea of doing a collection of Feghoots and he sent them to us, often in old copies of the original issues of *F&SF*, sometimes in yellowed manuscripts. As we went on, he kept finding more of them in his files.

We got the wonderful artist Tim Kirk to do the cover and some illustrations and we managed to get Reg a proof copy of the book right before he died in the summer of 1992.

As with everything with Reg, he was a very private person and we didn't even know he was ill. I'm just glad he got to see the book we did together. I sure hope he got a kick out of it.

Reg was one of those great writers that influenced so many things in the field of science fiction and fantasy from the late 1940s into and through the 1980s.

I feel stunningly honored to have gotten to know him, talk with him, and work with him. And at times still to this day forty years later, something comes up and reminds me of his great talent, his old-world manners and style, and his deep belly laugh.

Wow, he loved to laugh.

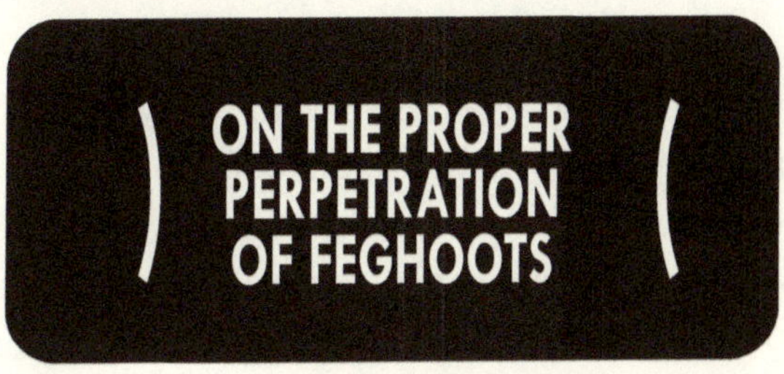

REGINALD BRETNOR

It may seem outrageous to speak of "perpetrating" a Feghoot—at least as outrageous as perpetrating a van Dyke, a Turner, a Mozart sonata, or any other generally recognized art form; and indeed, in using the term, I am simply truckling* to the vulgar notion (especially prevalent among academically influenced intellectuals) that puns and spoonerisms are always an abysmally low "form of wit.

Granted, then, that the Feghoot (or, if you will, feghoot) is an art form. Essentially, what does it entail?

The Feghoot (upper or lower case) is a short story—a short, short, short story—like any other short story (and I am speaking here of the sort of stories written by, say, John Collier, O. Henry, de Maupassant, Saki, and other masters of the form, not what the *New Yorker* and its "little magazine" imitators now consider the short story to be, an artificial slice of life as sensitive as an open wound, as circumscribed as a garotte, as amorphous as Los Angeles).

The proper short story, then, should contain nothing unnecessary to its telling. None of its elements, no matter how artistic, belongs in it unless its abstraction would either weaken or destroy it as a story, and the shorter the story, the more important this principle becomes. It is perhaps best illustrated by the short short story of, say, less than two thousand words. A beautiful example is Richard Condon's wonderful

"The Revenge of Harlow Funk," published many years ago in *Collier's*. Everything in it is essential, every bit of characterization, of description, of dialogue, contributes to the ending which is its raison d'etre.

All that is true of the short story and the short short story is doubly true of the shortest of them all, the limerick—and especially the bawdy limerick—and of those structured puns and spoonerisms which include feghoots.

Limericks provide what is probably the clearest illustration of what I mean, and there is one especially which I myself consider probably the most perfect in its genre:

There was a young architect, Rorick,
Who when feeling especially euphoric,
Could produce for inspection
Three kinds of erection—
Ionic, Corinthian, and Doric.

Nothing can be added to it that would improve it. Nothing can be subtracted from it that would not ruin it.

Neither the limerick nor the feghoot, of course, has to have a "surprise" ending. The ending is the capstone, and in achieving the desired effect the aim should be to find those words the goal demands—and this means exactly those words and no more. This is the reason why the writing of limericks, feghoots, and spoonerisms is such an excellent exercise for the short story writer and indeed for writers in general. It helps to develop the habit of not going hog wild at the typewriter and not trying to substitute torrents of words for clarity, strength, and ordered structure.

One of the feghootian beauties of the English language is that, while it is not overloaded with homonyms (like Japanese) it does have enough of them, and of their near kin, to make occasional multiple feghoots—often most pleasing of all—easier to achieve. So far as I know, too, both the limerick and the feghoot are solely English language phenomena, though I can't see why they necessarily should be. (After all, if "The Jabberwock" can be translated into French, German, Latin, and Greek—as it has been—who knows when we may find both limericks and feghoots emerging in, say, Magyar or Polish or Swahili?)

The rules for writing good feghoots are few and simple:

1. Never use an invented name or contrived word to make it come out.

2. Never run it to an excessive word length to make it come out. This betrays the inept would-be feghooter. All my own feghoots—with the exception of a few multiple ones—have run from about twenty to perhaps twenty-six double-spaced lines.

And here I repeat the real lesson of feghoot perpetration. If you accept its simple disciplines, you'll find it immensely helpful as a short story writer or—many New York editors perhaps to the contrary—even as a novelist, simply because these rules will force you, pleasantly but persistently, to choose the right words and only the right words, and to use no more of them than is necessary.

A truckling is not just a little truck. If it were, Toyota would be selling them.

FEGHOOT 1

In 2778, Ferdinand Feghoot landed on Dallas XIX, a previously unknown planet. He and his crew were immediately seized by the natives, trussed, and carried to a nearby veterinary hospital for investigation.

Lying there in the operating theater, the horrified crew saw a Dallasian nine feet high towering over their captain. He (the Dallasian) was as shaggy as a Kodiak bear. From the crown of his mushroom-shaped head grew a hand-like appendage holding a huge hypodermic full of fuming green fluids.

They started to scream out a warning. But they suddenly stopped—their captain had chuckled. They stared at him openmouthed. He grinned back.

"No need to get scared," said Ferdinand Feghoot. "It's just a furry with a syringe on top."

Soon after *A Budget of Musings Afloat and Ashore*, by "An Old Salt," appeared in 3412, Vice-Admiral Sir Trumpery Buckett invited Ferdinand Feghoot to visit the 18th Century and meet Madame Pompadour. Though his manner seemed odd, Feghoot accepted; and they left via the)(at the Time-Travellers Club.

To Feghoot's surprise, they emerged not in France, but on a dark London street where a mob was storming and roaring.

"Feghoot," Sir Trumpery gloated, "I have trapped you. That was my book you reviewed. You called it a 'a slop chest of moth-eaten jottings, a dull, ill-assorted olla podrida.' Well—" He pointed to the oncoming mob. "—here's my revenge! These are the Gordon Riots, my boy—the zenith of British anti-Catholicism. You have boasted that nothing can force you to utter a bigoted word against any religion. Ha! You will now . . . if you want to survive!" And he roared with laughter.

"DOWN WITH PRIESTS! PAPISTS GO HOME!" the mob bellowed.

A huge Scotsman came up, brandishing billhook and torch—and Feghoot at once began yelling as loudly as anyone else.

"I thought so," Sir Trumpery sneered. "This will make a fine story."

"But I'm not against any religion—I'm denouncing your miserable book! NO POTPOURRI!" shouted Ferdinand Feghoot.

FEGHOOT 3

In 7884, Ferdinand Feghoot invented and marketed Dr. Feghoot's Golden Medical Discovery, which raised all vertebrates to the intelligence level of the average TV viewer. This caused an unemployment problem of major proportions. Eventually, though, the new citizens went to work in factories or offices, hired out as domestics, or were blanketed into the civil service. Only the ducks could find no jobs at all.

They appealed to Ferdinand Feghoot himself, who solved the problem at once. It was the custom for people to send themselves greetings on important occasions. After that, when nightingales, thrushes, and other Western Union employees went out to sing greetings like these, a duck went along with the bill.

It was only fitting that Ferdinand Feghoot should get the first of them all on his two hundred and twelfth birthday. The lark messenger sang, "Many happy returns of the day, dear Ferdinand," several times; and then the duck extended his beak with the bill.

"Ah!" Ferdinand Feghoot said with a smile. "A duck-billed platitude!"

FEGHOOT 4

In 2916, after a captivity of twenty-two years, Ferdinand Feghoot escaped from the planet Aah-ook. As soon as he landed on Earth, hundreds of reporters surrounded him and began asking questions, which he answered with his usual directness:

"The Aah-ookians are highly intelligent dragonoid beings upwards of eight hundred yards long."

"I was taken by one called Urk-tss. He was so old that he had a full set of false teeth, uppers and lowers. Each plate measured at least fifty yards front to back."

"No, he treated me very humanely. My only task was to take the seeds out of the melons and things so that they wouldn't get under his teeth; and he went to great lengths to protect me from bat-weevils and other huge vermin. In fact, he had one of his molars hollowed out into a cozy three-room apartment, and allowed me to live there."

"You poor, dear man!" sighed a sob-sister. "How dread-ful—to be a slave all those years."

"A slave? Goodness, no!" replied Ferdinand Feghoot. "I was an indentured servant."

Ferdinand Feghoot explored the system of the star y-Turista during the Third Franco-Mexican Empire. The expedition was sponsored by His Cosmic Majesty Maximilliano Ixtlhuatl XXH, who decreed patriotically that only Mexican food might be served aboard ship.

In 3002, Feghoot returned, and was ushered directly into the Presence.

"What did you find?" asked the Emperor.

"Sire," replied, Feghoot, "most marvelous of all are our Ixixixangos." He pointed to a couple of creatures who looked like vitrified anteaters and clanked when they walked. "All other life-forms are either carbon or silicon based. Only the Ixixixango has a chemistry based upon both, and requires both for its substance."

"You mean they can't eat what everyone eats?"

"No indeed. We fed them ground glass and meat."

"Ha!" cried the Emperor. "So that's how you follow my orders, Fernando Feghoot. Ground-glass-and-meat isn't Mexican food!"

"It is too!" said Feghoot. "It's silicon carne."

In 3299, Ferdinand Feghoot took his youngest son to Hawaii 1960 for a real old-fashioned luau. They both wore aloha shirts, and their telepathic translator was disguised as a coconut. "Remember," warned Feghoot. "Do just what they do."

He adjusted the time-bulb to return in four hours—and presto! there they were. Sure enough, a big luau was in progress. But it wasn't a 1960 luau. The beach was crowded with naked Hawaiians armed with war clubs.

"Well, well—two more courses!" growled their king, who was wearing an antique British naval officer's coat.

Feghoot saw that a slight error had taken them back to 1779, just as their hosts were about to eat Captain Cook—who, indeed, smelled very savory. "We dropped in for potluck," he said quickly, trusting to traditional Hawaiian hospitality.

"We-ell, I guess we can spare a chop," grunted the king, passing a couple. "Mighty tasty too, I must say."

"But I don't want to eat humans!" piped up the boy.

It was a critical moment—but Ferdinand Feghoot handled it with his usual aplomb. "Go ahead, eat it," he said with a smile. "One man's meat is another man's poi, son."

In 3588, the space liner *Asimov Maru* was forced down on a seemingly unknown planet. Her interstellar transmitters were wrecked and her supplies were all ruined.

Her captain sought out Ferdinand Feghoot, who luckily was one of the passengers. "Please help us," he begged.

For a moment, Feghoot regarded the landscape. Then, "Bring baskets and a big iron griddle," he ordered. "Follow me!"

They obeyed. For hours, they trudged over burning sand and dry cactus. Finally, when they were close to despair, he pointed at an advancing wall of brown fog.

"I thought so!" he cried. "This planet is called Even Greater L.A. It is famous for its edible smog, which tastes just like mushrooms. Light a big fire. Heat up the griddle!" Beckoning to the men with the baskets, he drew his machete.

Soon the men were back with succulent chunks of the edible smog, and these he immediately threw on the fire. They jiggled and twitched; shrill cries seemed to come from them.

"Mr. Feghoot!" the captain exclaimed. "That isn't just smog. Th-the inhabitants seem to be in it!"

"Think nothing of it," laughed Ferdinand Feghoot. "It's all mist to my grill."

There was a great deal of ignorant opposition on Earth to Ferdinand Feghoot's Galactic Concordat of 2133, which made interstellar tourism universally possible.

Fortunately, Feghoot was present when the first tourist landed in Old Sanfran Cisco, right where a new office building was being constructed. The tourist was a striped, felinoid being from a planet called Mrrr-ow; except for his long double tail he looked like an overweight Bengal tiger. He paid no attention to Feghoot or to the nervous crowd which had gathered. He was interested only in the fence round the building, through which, until a few minutes previously, numerous sidewalk superintendents had been peering. He sat down beside it. He purred. He reached out a huge claw, hooked it into one of the holes in the fence, pulled out a piece of the succulent pine, munched it, and purred even more loudly. Then he repeated the process again and again.

A small, waspish woman dashed forward, carrying a sign which said, MONSTERS LEAVE OUR DAUGHTERS ALONE!!! "Kill it!" she screamed. "Nobody ever saw anything like it before!"

An ugly murmur came from the crowd—but Ferdinand Feghoot rose neatly to the occasion. "Nonsense," he laughed. "It's nothing to be afraid of. It's only a purr-pull peephole eater."

The Ismaili Institute of Higher Studies always rewarded the annual Hayworth Memorial Lecturer with his weight in diamonds—but only if he withstood the attacks of the faculty. Ferdinand Feghoot, lecturing on "Space Colonization and the Human Emotions," ran this gauntlet successfully in 2883.

"Everywhere man has gone," he declared, "and no matter how he has changed, you always find some small, homey, nostalgic reminder of old Mother Earth."

At once he was challenged. "What about the planet Candide?" a professor demanded. "They are infidels, cannibals! How could anything there remind one of Earth?"

For an instant, Feghoot was taken aback. Then he smiled. "I would have said you were right," he replied, "if it hadn't been for one thing. As you know, the Candideans especially relish the plump juicy buttocks of slaves raised on large farms for the purpose. And it was on one of these farms that I saw something which took me right back to my boyhood, and brought tears to my eyes."

"What was it?" everyone asked.

"It stood on a shelf in the kitchen," sighed Ferdinand Feghoot. "It was just an old Fanny Farmer Cook Book."

It was Ferdinand Feghoot who discovered Yip Quang and persuaded him to move to the Thirty-Ninth Century.

"Mr. Yip," he informed the Time-Travellers Club, "is the greatest natural psychokineticist in all history. He put every Chinese laundry in Milwaukee 1912 out of business. He hired no help. He needed no plant or equipment. He simply sat down before a mountain of dirty old laundry, and wished it all clean, ironed, sorted, and wrapped. He closed his eyes for a moment—and pop! it was done. In no time at all he'd made millions of dollars."

Old Dr. Gropius Volkswagen rose to his feet. "Then why is he here?" he demanded unpleasantly. "Why did he not stay where he was so happy and rich?"

"He was rich but not happy," Feghoot answered. "His fellow Chinese weren't at all fond of him. Some of them snubbed him completely, and none of them ever invited him anywhere."

"That is strange. The Chinese worshipped commercial success. Did he commit some unforgivable crime? Did he violate some precept of maybe Confucius?"

"Oh, no," said Ferdinand Feghoot. "It was nothing like that. It was just that they found him a little too wishy-washy."

It was Ferdinand Feghoot who, in 3312, first proved that fish were highly intelligent and that men could converse with them. He was accorded the honor of signing the ensuing Treaty of Peace, Amity, Commerce, and Navigation—which was also endorsed by an imposing elderly shark.

"I spent seventeen months eavesdropping on fish conversations and analyzing their language," he told reporters after the ceremony. "Then I slipped overboard with my skin-diving gear, and asked for their leader. They took me to the Generalissimo here, and I'll never forget my first sight of him, completely at ease in the lovely blue water, with that busy little fish hovering right by his head all the time. He received me most courteously in spite of my abominable accent. Why, he was so polite and so tactful that it was almost a week before I realized that he is as deaf as a post."

"But—how could he understand you?" asked the reporters.

"That's simple," said Ferdinand Feghoot. "The little fish is his herring aide."

Ferdinand Feghoot was a close friend of the Very Reverend William Ralph Inge. His time shuttle was installed in a back bedroom of St. Paul's Deanery, and the Gloomy Dean knew perfectly well that he came from the future. (Indeed, his tale of coming events was largely responsible for the nickname.)

"My boy," the Dean said one day, "couldn't we take a jaunt in your time machine? I'd like to talk with John Donne, the great poet. lie was Dean of St. Paul's too, you know."

Feghoot acceded. He rented Dean Inge an appropriate costume and took him back to 1624; where, after explaining the situation to Donne, who was vastly amused, he left them alone for a full day of discussion. The effect on Donne became obvious only a week later.

"Fferdinand Ffeghoote," demanded King James I, "what's awry? There's not a merry word from John Donne. Last night he read a Devotion full only of funerals and death. He said, 'Never send to ask for whom the bell tolls; it tolls for thee.' Aye, as gloomy as that! What makes him choose such a subject?"

"Your Majesty," said Ferdinand Feghoot, "you know how these great poets are—give 'em an Inge and they take a knell."

In 2961, Ferdinand Feghoot persuaded the Council of Worlds to admit Little Stravinsky. After Dr. Hassan ben-Sabah had finished denouncing that planet, he said:

"Gentlemen, our learned colleague has accused the Little Stravinskians of 'the utmost barbarity'—even though they have achieved automation and space travel. Why? Because they cling to their old, picturesque customs. They shackle their King to his throne with a Chain of Gold which is their equivalent of the Crown. Every year, they choose fifty singers with seven-stringed harps to serve this Chain, as they put it, entertaining the Monarch with ballads and lays. At the end of each year, they have a great contest in which the singers belabor each other with whips until the last one on his feet gets the Grand Prize. Well, what of it?"

"The Grand Prize is a beautiful virgin!" screamed Dr. ben-Sabah. "She is called Miss Little Stravinsky of, say, 2961. The winner gets her for his concubine. It is shocking! Immoral! Uncivilized! Nothing like this ever happened on Earth!"

"Nonsense!" laughed Ferdinand Feghoot. "Why, we even have an old saying: Bards of a fetter flog to get 'er."

Ferdinand Feghoot was once Emperor of China, ruling as Fei Hu (357-329 B.C.). Arriving as a time tourist, be was so much taken with the court ladies that he chose to remain; and the aged Emperor, struck by his wisdom, quickly adopted him.

His reign was one of great splendor, and it was only in its twenty-eighth year that be sadly called back his chronoscooter.

It appeared as one of those miniature clouds seen in Chinese scroll paintings. He mounted it before his whole court.

"Son of Heaven," wept his Prime Minister, "though you ascend on the Dragon, your innumerable children enrich us. You have mentioned your red-haired cousin. We beg you, send him to rule us and beget many more children like these!"

As Feghoot had a lot of blond genes, his children really stood out from the crowd. Because this had aroused so much envy and caused them endless puzzlement and distress, he had decided to abdicate. So he shook his head firmly.

"But we need more of them," cried the Minister. "Think of their great Filial Piety. They are headed along the True Way!"

"No," said Ferdinand Feghoot. "I must leave you my Tao-headed children—but my cousin would make Confucians even worse confounded."

In August 3188, Ferdinand Feghoot saved Earth from a trans-temporal invasion by the Thutians, an uncouth race from the wrong side of the Coalsack. Learning of their intentions, he presented himself at their Chief of Staff's office disguised as a Martian mroof trader. These persons having been everywhere, he was cordially welcomed. The Chief of Staff asked him at once whether Earth 1970 had anything better than primitive nuclear weapons.

Feghoot extruded his (synthetic) third-eye-stalk, as all Martians do when they want to be very impressive. "Earth 1970," he declared, "has the most terrible weapons ever developed. Its scientists take certain common, virtually harmless airborne germs, speed up their reproduction tremendously, concentrate them in fantastic numbers, and direct them at individuals and groups of the enemy, who are infallibly doomed."

The Chief of Staff turned very pale. "Wh-what do they call

th-these abominable weapons?" he asked.

"Guided measles," whispered Ferdinand Feghoot.

It was in 3008 that Ferdinand Feghoot, single-handed, rescued the Reverend Mahatma G. Birdshot from the primitive humanoids of the planet called Egg, who had decided to kill him.

The Eggians took to Feghoot at once. They brought him fresh fish, fruit, and strong native beer. They gave him a bevy of their fattest, most beautiful maidens to dance the notorious erotic dances of Egg for his benefit. And they told him indignantly that their King was enraged with the missionary because he had turned down these traditional gifts with contempt.

Every day, from his prison, the Reverend Birdshot saw Feghoot disporting himself with the dancing girls—especially with one, plumper than any, and the most expert performer of all, who was getting all sorts of special attentions, meals-between-meals and high-calorie tidbits. Finally he could stand it no longer. "Libertine!" he cried out. "Go back to Earth! I would rather be martyred than accept rescue from you! What are you doing to that poor girl? Are you preparing her to serve your base lusts?"

"Hush, dear Brother," replied Ferdinand Feghoot. "I am doing this only for you. I am fattening her up to send back to the King. Remember—a stuffed dancer turneth away wrath."

To the despair of his crew, Ferdinand Feghoot remained on the planet Chroma from 3357 to 3361.

"Please, sir," they begged. "We know how fine it must be to see all those Chromatid ladies come marching in with their cute little egg-sacs for the Communal Hatch every five years. We know that each generation is all of one color—fuchsia or mauve or dark green, or whatever—and that bright, solid colors are especially esteemed; and we'd like to be in on the betting. But all of it's only biology, sir. What'll become of us when we go back to Earth without having made any cultural discoveries?"

It was futile. When the great Hatch took place, Feghoot shouted his joy as loudly as any Chromatid in the stadium as an unprecedentedly lovely new generation burst out of its shells.

He collected his winnings, returned directly to Earth, and was straightaway summoned before the Gardener-General.

"Feghoot!" roared the ruler, whetting his pruning hook. "How can my garden grow without art, without culture? In five years, you have seen no new painting, no new sculpture, not even any new taxidermy! I must prune you!"

"You are misinformed, Verdant Majesty," said Ferdinand Feghoot. "I was present at the Birth of the Blues."

(with thanks to Charles G. Leedbam)

Ferdinand Feghoot almost introduced modern golf into Scotland in the reign of William the Lion (1165–1214). His time-taxi stalled, and he had to step out with his clubs. He quickly persuaded the King that he wasn't a wizard, and soon he was ordered to teach the whole court how to play.

He was given as servants all the common folk in Dunfermline, where the links were to be. They graded, ploughed, weeded, seeded, watered, and mowed. Soon, he announced the grand opening. The armorers worked overtime on mashies and niblicks, and his servants celebrated so riotously in advance that the Monarch, wakened by their noise, had all the younger ones mercilessly beaten.

After breakfast, the procession moved out; and the King at first expressed satisfaction. Then he saw huge, hairy Highlanders carrying the clubs. "Ha!" he cried. "You told me the caddies would be the fairest youths of my realm!" He pointed at some boys and young men nursing their bruises. "Tell them to carry our clubs."

"Your Majesty," said Ferdinand Feghoot, "those are the lads you had beaten last night. They are quite black and blue. So sore are they I doubt they can walk. Wise though I be"—he drew himself up—"I cannot free the sorest for the tees!"

(with thanks to Victor J. Papanek)

In 3180, Ferdinand Feghoot found the planet called Pigg. It was worthy of note, not because all its species were civilized (which is common enough), but because the spirits of its dead remained visibly present for years, getting into the same sorts of scrapes they had when alive. This troubled the living, who were convinced that there was no way to help or console them.

Feghoot saw an example as he was taking a stroll with the President. A little ghost-cat crept up, weeping and wailing.

"Th-th-that old gh-gh-ghost B-Boxer bit off my t-t-t-tail!" he told them, sobbing and blowing his nose.

"Oh dear, dear, dear!" the President moaned. "And there's nothing at all we can do!"

Feghoot paid no attention. Kneeling, he whispered some words. Instantly, the ghost-cat leaped happily up, thanked him politely, and dashed off purring a tune.

"How splendid!" the President cried. "Mr. Feghoot, what did you say?"

"I told him to go to a grog shop."

"A grog shop, but why?"

"Because," said Ferdinand Feghoot, "that is where they retail spirits."

FEGHOOT 20

Ferdinand Feghoot produced the greatest horror movies of all time in the late 1970s. He discovered the dreadful Karkas Gabor working as an obscure undertaker's assistant in Budapest; and his werewolves, vampires, zombies, bakemono, and things that went bump in the night were so real that he was threatened with several exorcisms and a Congressional Investigation. Then Karkas Gabor was murdered.

The suspects were obvious: Basil Dripp-Grue, with his extra-long eyeteeth and his corpse-like mistress, Evila de Kay; old, hairy-palmed Lou Garou; petite Liz Bathory, who seemed to have come out of nowhere, and her boyfriend, the gibbering Orson J. Papaloi; and a great many creepy-crawlies who starred in the worst sort of B pictures. All were fiendishly jealous of Gabor.

The police questioned one and another, and got nowhere. Then Dripp-Grue and Evila gave Feghoot the one clue he needed. They invited everyone in the vampire-werewolf set to a banquet and served up poor Gabor, whom they had murdered and cremated, disguised in a stew. At once, Feghoot had them arrested.

"It was simple," he told the admiring audience. "If you had my experience with Transylvanian cuisine, you too would be able to recognize Hungarian ghoul ash."

(with thanks to Laurence Gurney)

When Ferdinand Feghoot was rejuvenated in 4128, a slight error brought him out as an apple-cheeked boy of eleven. As such he was legally an incompetent orphan, and his guardians procured him a berth as midshipman in the Space Navy.

The hard-bitten crew made him the butt of many practical jokes. However, on the planet Galumph, when they took him out snipe-hunting, he returned with a sackful of snipe. And in the Scanderberg System, ordered to locate a spacestretcher, he contacted the first Uilliu ship ever seen—just full of the gadgets, which the Uilliuub had invented as a meteor defense. Finally a tricky old CPO popped him into a lifeboat and sent him to Earth on an impossible errand.

Feghoot returned six weeks later—and with him were a dozen young female apes. These rushed forward at once, eagerly trying to shake hands with the Captain, who was thoroughly angry.

"My word!" the Chaplain exclaimed. "Look at them, sir. Not one of them is right-handed—every one is a southpaw!"

The Captain ignored him. "Explain yourself, Mr. Feghoot!" he roared.

"I was only obeying the Chief Bosun's orders," lisped Ferdinand Feghoot in his childish treble. "He sent me for some left-handed monkey wenches."

(with thanks to Dan Kelly)

It was Ferdinand Feghoot's inflexible logic which, in 3938, succeeded in tempering the barbarous colonial oppressions of Chunder-ud-Din, All-Powerful Lord108 of Hindustan, Earth, and the Outlying Worlds, Son of the Prophet, and Official Reincarnation of Pandit Nehru, Maria Callas, and Bishop G. Bromley Oxnam.

On the conquered planet Saddhu XVI, which was singularly Earthlike, the Autocrat saw the important role played by Great Auks, which were by no means extinct, in the culture. The natives buried their dead in large cairns with lids of baked clay, and in the hurricane season this gave rise to mournful organ-like sounds which were blamed on spirits lamenting the presence of insects infesting their graves. Therefore families who could afford it hung a Great Auk in a cage under the lid of their cairn, feeding it regularly. The birds were fair windstoppers, but the tribal elders believed that they went down at night and picked bugs off the corpses.

As Grand Vizier, Feghoot explained all this very carefully. But the ruler was outraged. "Why don't they expose their dead for the vultures to eat, like civilized people?" he cried out. "Wipe them out! There's no precedent for this sort of custom."

"Precedent?" exclaimed Ferdinand Feghoot. "O Thrice-Born, have you not heard about 'Great Auks from lid allay cairn's groan?'"

(with thanks to Leonard Rubin)

In 3270, Ferdinand Feghoot's star-drive broke down while he and a person named Lodowick Goor were serving as Couriers for the Greater Galactic Th'lgian Empire. With the ship helplessly drifting, he struggled to make the repairs. In three weeks the food was exhausted, and they faced seemingly certain starvation. Soon the unhappy Goor was eyeing the diplomatic pouch hungrily.

Th'lgian tradition demanded that all official dispatches be written on xx'tti, which when boiled tastes simply delicious to all known life-forms. Terrans, however, were so vulnerable to alien diseases that even out in deep space they were forbidden to eat any foods not grown on Earth. Violators were stripped of their citizenship and perpetually exiled from their native planet. That was why the Th'lgi trusted Earthmen as Imperial Couriers.

Goor had, of course, been solemnly warned—but hunger was too much for the man. On the fifth day, while Feghoot was working, he sneaked the dispatches into the galley, boiled them, and devoured them greedily.

Feghoot, returning after having repaired the drive, saw at once what had happened. He stared at his shipmate in pity and horror. "Goor!" he cried out. "Do you know what you've done? You have sold your Earthright for a pot of message!"

FEGHOOT 24

Ferdinand Feghoot placed himself in great peril when he explored the dry-jungle valleys of Golightly III, and discovered the *dzop*, the strange flying bird-plants that breed there. The indigenous aborigines killed every stranger, stuffed him with *dzop* feather-leaves, and set him up as one of their innumerable charms. To get by, Feghoot had to pose as an almost omnipotent charm-maker, and everything went along nicely until the start of the dzop egg-laying season, which was sacred. Then the Queen came to see him.

"Mighty Magician," she said, "we have always wanted charms made out of *dzop* eggs, but we have never had them because they travel too fast. You are powerful. You will be able to catch them."

Dzop egg sacs were modified seed-pods, and great pressure built up inside them. Finally, when the flocks found their meaty blue nest-trees, this became unendurable. Each *dzop* aimed its tail at its tree, and let go. The eggs broke out of their sacs at a velocity of over 2800 feet per second, and buried themselves deep in the trees, where they eventually hatched.

"Well?" said the Queen, gnashing her eighty-one teeth. Ferdinand Feghoot did some quick thinking. "Of course I could catch them, Your Highness," he answered, "but you can't make an amulet with out-breaking eggs."

Ferdinand Feghoot, accompanied by his then youngest son, aged eight, rediscovered the curious planet of RoboCathay in 7282. He told the boy how its mechanical wonders had been created by refugees from what had been Communist China millennia before, and how man had abandoned it to the robots during the Thousand Year Plague. He showed him how these robots had preserved all the customs of their long-vanished masters, especially Confucius' moral doctrine of filial piety, which was still their whole basis of law. Then, so that the lesson of this robotic respect for one's elders should not be lost on the boy, he took him to see the Law Courts of Robo-Cathay.

They watched while a little machine was tried for "the most shameful unfilial behavior to its parent machine." The little machine, which was designed to hold pieces of metal while the big machine worked on them, had very rudely refused.

"Papa, I don't understand," piped up young Feghoot, as the Judge prepared to pass sentence. "What does it mean? What's wrong with the little machine?"

"My boy," said Ferdinand Feghoot, "it's a vise child that noes its own father."

(with thanks to Lenore Sellers)

Ferdinand Feghoot was the only man to hold a high rank in the Navy during the Missourian Momarchy (2504–2622 A.D.). He actually attained supreme command, flying the flag of High Admiral of the Blue, and so ranking all the female High Admirals. Except in one case, his tact and personal charm at once dissolved all jealousy and ill-feeling.

This exception was his immediate subordinate, an old seadog named Hattie McBoom. Her resentment came to a climax when Feghoot was issued a smart admiral's barge six feet longer than hers and with space for four additional oars-women. At its first appearance, she ordered her main batteries to fire on it, and sank it with a number of casualties.

She was arrested at once, a Naval Court was convened, and its unanimous verdict was announced within twenty minutes—she was to be keelhauled, then hanged from the yardarm. Her life was saved by High Admiral Feghoot, who, despite his own narrow escape, eloquently pleaded for leniency, stating that the case was clearly a psychiatric one.

"What do you mean, Sir?" cried the President of the Court.

"It's obvious, Madame," answered Ferdinand Feghoot. "We have here a simple case of old-fashioned pinnace envy."

In 2263, Ferdinand Feghoot and his beautiful wife landed on Blaupunkt, a backwoods planet where thousands of construction hands, crewmen, and scientists had been marooned for six years. They at once fell madly in love with her. Luckily, one of their scientists had perfected a matter duplicator which could duplicate living beings as easily as ten-credit bills. The duplicates were shy on intelligence, but the Feghoots' hosts didn't care in the least. Very politely, they asked Mrs. Feghoot to act as their model, and amiably she agreed.

Because the duplicator could turn out only a dozen women a day, polyandry was resorted to. Each new woman was married to a gang of ten men. The gangs prized their wives highly, and treated them well; and the good-natured duplicates enjoyed the arrangement tremendously.

Soon, however, Mrs. Feghoot began to lose weight and feel tired and irritable. "Every time they marry one of those girls, it takes something out of me," she complained. "Ferdinand, take me away!"

Feghoot watched for his chance. Slamming the air-lock of his spaceship when all the men were outside, he prepared to take off.

The men pleaded and wept. "Please don't go yet," they begged.

"I'm sorry," Ferdinand Feghoot said sadly, "but those wedding gangs are breaking up that old belle of mine."

(with thanks to David Burwasser)

Dr. Gropius Volkswagen, the philologist, was the one man who disliked Ferdinand Feghoot's ravishing cousin, Isabeau Feghoot. "Isabeau indeed!" he would grumble. "What does it matter if her mother was time-travelling, and so she was born long ago when Henry VIII or Harry the Trueman ruled Missouri and England? She should be Isabelle. Isabeau is archaic!"

Isabeau paid no attention. When Ferdinand warned her that the old man was dangerously brooding, she just giggled.

Then one evening they found Dr. Volkswagen lying in wait for them with a blunderbuss. "Ha-ha!" he cried wildy. "Now I show you! To use obsolete names is a very bad habit. Take paper, a pencil! You must write, first archaic one thousand times—then, one thousand times, It is a bad habit. Write."

They wrote, wrote, and wrote. When they had finished, with Isabeau nearly in tears, he ordered them to wad up the papers. "Now I, Gropius Volkswagen, will make you eat up your words. Begin!"

He waited until they had finished. "Well," he crowed, "will that teach you not to use Isabeau? Does it not prove you wrong?"

"Not at all," replied Ferdinand Feghoot. "It just shows that we're a remarkable family. We can eat archaic and habit too."

(with thanks to M. T. Cicero McIntyre)

In 3229, when Ferdinand Feghoot arose to deliver his famous report to the Society for the Aesthetic Rearrangement of History, his reception was hostile.

"Feghoot," cried Dr. Corydon Bramahpootra, the President, "is it not the purpose of our Society to make all history Classically perfect, as though Gibbon himself had composed it?—to change every event that is crude, inartistic? When we sent you back to the early 1960s, did we not ask you to avert the untidy Sino-Indian War?"

He gave Feghoot no chance to reply. "We did! And every day a Learned Commission examined the texts to see if they'd changed. Vast sums were wagered on your success; duels were actually fought. And what did you accomplish? At the peak of the crisis, you arranged for ex-Premier Castro of Cuba to visit Prime Minister Nehru! You even mismanaged that, so that Castro wandered all over India sight-seeing while his host waited for him in vain, getting more and more angry!"

Imperturbably, Feghoot nodded.

"Wretch!" screeched the Doctor. "You have betrayed our ideals! Was that in the Classical spirit of Gibbon?"

"Of course it was," answered Ferdinand Feghoot. "Now I can tell you how, as the fate of the world hung in the balance, Fidel roamed while Nehru burned."

It was Ferdinand Feghoot who saved one of Civilization's noblest works of piety and learning—the great *Summa Theologica* of St. Thomas Aquinas—for posterity.

In 4282, the Cardinal-Prefect of Alternate Time Tracks told him that young Thomas, instead of studying hard, was succumbing to an earthly temptation—a seemingly innocent one smuggled to him by a time-traveling Occamist agent from the 34th Century.

Immediately, Feghoot went back to 1541 and the castle of San Giovanni, where the youth was being kept prisoner by misguided relatives. In the guise of an abbot, he gained admittance—and found Thomas luxuriating in a lovely, hot bubble bath, which two guards kept replenishing.

"My son," he exclaimed, "do you not know that a holy hermit has prophesied a great future for you? What are you doing?"

"I'm simply wallowing in this heavenly bath," sighed the lad. "Father, it's wonderful. I could lie here forever."

Then Ferdinand Feghoot drew himself up to his full height and pronounced the words which at once set things straight.

"You must not!" he cried out in an awful voice. "Remember, Thomas Aquinas—one's wallow does not make a summa!"

It was Ferdinand Feghoot who saved the Mulch Expedition on Rumjungle III in 3449. Because the planet's intelligent race dreaded gadgets and hated all strangers, the Expedition could use only native equipment—semi-intelligent, specialized fauna the Rumjunglians carried in their carapace-pouches. Instead of a compass, they employed a stick-insect which pointed due North on command.

Two weeks out, with the nearest waterhole a hundred miles off, the guides came up rustling politely. "Now this is our egg-whistling time, for the spore-sounds," they declared. "We go now. But you safe, Big Soft Bipeds. We leave point-to-North insect. Very fine, one year guaranteed. Goodbye, thank you." After giving instructions on how to make the thing work, they vanished into the darkness.

For another week, the expedition advanced. Then they found that the stick-insect was pointing everywhere except North. They were lost. "But everything's all right," said Professor Hudibras Mulch. "The natives explained. Stick-insects always do this for eight or ten days in the rutting-season. We'll wait. We'll have just enough water."

"No!" Feghoot cried. "I'll pick up a lodestone instead. It's a plot. Look at that insect—they've given us one that's insane!"

"Insane? B-but how can you tell?"

"It's obvious," said Ferdinand Feghoot. "Non-compass mantis."

In 3285, Ferdinand Feghoot solved the famous riddle of the graffiti of Amis, the Planet of Ruins.

"Imagine it!" cried his friend, Arch-Archaeologist Kingsley. "Thousands of scholars have tried to elucidate them, all in vain! Even I have only been able to identify the components. That stylized female figure clearly portrays the legendary Abigail Penfold, a woman from Kent in the old Earth country of England. She is said to have made a vast fortune by preserving unwanted seabirds in tins and shipping them out to space settlers, who considered them luxuries. Even today, her name is a by-word, like Hot Dog Harry's on Earth. But it's the upper half of the thing that's driving me mad! Look! There are three lions, not heraldic at all, but just sitting there smugly, as serene as you please. Feghoot, what have they to do with the old girl and her tins?"

Feghoot regarded the drawings for nearly a minute. "I believe," he declared, "that these refer to an archaic English poem." The Arch-Archaeologist smiled condescendingly.

"I can't document it," said Ferdinand Feghoot. "I'm afraid you'll have to accept it for what my word's worth. But it's really quite simple. Those are lions, composed, above Tinned-Tern Abby."

(with thanks to Martin Graetz)

Ferdinand Feghoot was the greatest irrigation engineer in all history. He brought water to Mars by diverting icebergs from the trans-Plutonian asteroid belts. He piped fresh ammonia to the deserts of Capella XIII, where valuable crystalline music-plants grow. He almost settled the water dispute between Northern and Southern Calfunya.

But his hardest task came on Lushmeadow Acres, a small planet sold to a colony of New Amish by Good-as-Gold Gaazreeb, a Vegan promoter. The arable land lay at over 10,000 feet; the water at sea-level. "Our religion forbids us machinery," the settlers explained. "We can afford only one more cargo from Earth. In six months, Good-as-Gold will foreclose. Save us, Ferdinand Feghoot!"

Feghoot took charge. He ordered the final cargo, and he started the colonists channeling and digging. When Gaazreeb came with his bailiffs, rivers were flowing uphill all over the planet, every field was loaded with crops, and the bank had refinanced.

"How did you do it?" screamed Gaazreeb, using every one of his voice ducts. He pointed at the tide from the fresh-water sea, running into a river bed. "No machine! Water flows over pickles!"

"Naturally," smiled Ferdinand Feghoot. "That was our cargo. We've known it for centuries on Earth. Dill waters run steep."

(with thanks to Capt. E.D. Hams)

In 2927, Ferdinand Feghoot rescued Vaila, a minor planet in the Hebridean System, from a plague of rats who had left a doomed Cassiopeian freighter. On Vaila, no cat could live, so nothing threatened them. "What can we do, sir?" asked the Laird.

"You can make robot cats," Feghoot answered. He designed them, and the natives began turning them out. They killed rat after rat; and the sight of them, in their plastic, striped-tabby skins, cheered everyone up. Success was in sight, and a great celebration was being prepared, when word came of a frightening mutation—a pair of huge rats who were devouring the cats.

"They will reproduce!" moaned the Laird. "We are lost!"

"Not at all," Feghoot said; and he built one last cat. It had no sleek plastic coat. Instead, it was covered with a poor grade of enamel, like an old chamber pot. Almost at once, a mutant rat saw it and caught it. It was tough, but the rat chewed and chewed. Finally it swallowed—and huge, jagged fragments of the shoddy enamel came loose in its stomach. Soon it died in great agony.

"Wonderful!" cried the overjoyed Laird. "But what happened?"

"He strained at a cat, and swallowed enamel," said Ferdinand Feghoot.

(with thanks to Edward Truscoe)

It was because of an argument with Ferdinand Feghoot that Richard Wagner was convicted of plagiarism in 2867. On a visit to Bayreuth, Feghoot had told him about the planet Madamabutterfry in the Twenty-Ninth Century, and how the natives believed that every grand opera idea had been stolen from them, and how they invariably proved it. Instantly, Wagner flew into a fury. "Only Teutonic ideas are goot for Grand Opera!" he stormed. "The rest iss all rubbish! Get your mazhine for shpace-time. Ve go to your planet. I vill show you!"

On Madamabutterfry, the Customs officials asked whether Wagner had anything to declare—any operas, acts, scenes, or arias—and he sneeringly gave them a list. Within minutes, they had him arrested, and a police official was offering to show him the themes he had pilfered.

Right at the spaceport, he was led to a vast, ancient tree with eye-buds and tentacle-tendrils. Every leaf drooped; its bark was dull, dry, and scaly; it rustled hopelessly at them. Near it was a pile of used spaceship parts and a sign saying:

ROOTBOTTOM STANLEY, THE EARTHMAN'S FRIEND!

BEST DEAL IN THE GALAXY!! ABSOLUTELY NO BEING UNDERSELLS ME!!

GARFINKLES, TOP QUALITY 17.95! TODAY ONLY 8.95!

NEVER AGAIN! 1.97!!!

Nearby was a little booth manned by a small, molelike person; its sign said simply:

GARFINKLES, SIX FOR A DIME.

"So tragic," murmured the policeman, "such a valuable theme."

"But vodt could I have written aboudt it?" roared Wagner.

"That's obvious," Feghoot said. "Tree Stan Undersold."

They went on to a cook shop, where their escort showed them an enormous jar full of jam. Stretched over its top was a flat, rubbery organism with two mournful eyes and a mouth in the middle.

"Such a sadness," lamented the policeman, dabbing away at a tear. "With hunger he grasps at the jar, and so does his work. But if he is fed, then he will let go and sleep."

"Can't I please have some jam?" called a thin little voice. "Just a nibble, just one. Oh, how I long for it!"

"I suspect," remarked Feghoot before Wagner could speak, "that this is the Nibble-longing Lid."

Finally they were brought to the edge of an odorous bog, where a huge, froglike person was unhappily tying oysters to strings and dropping them into the water to marinate them.

His topknot glowed fitfully with a faint, sickly light.

"This is the most tragic of all," said the policeman. "Very artistic, nice to steal. No one buys now his bivalves. That is why his light-on-top cannot shine."

"An oudraitch!" screamed Wagner, leaping and frothing and tearing his hair. "It iss ridiculous! Vot iss this to me?"

"Dim Oyster Sinker," said Ferdinand Feghoot.

The Women's Absolute Equality Party elected its first President in 2482, and set out to take over all known planets.

Ferdinand Feghoot, then Governor-General of Awk-k-k-kaw in the system of Aldebaran, was ordered to accept a Mrs. Taffypull Jihad as his "Instructress," to give her all aid while she indoctrinated the intelligent aviform natives, and finally resign his office.

Mrs. Jihad taught the Awk-k-k-kawians exactly how things were done back on Earth, not only in politics but in everything else. Her pupils were apt; and she soon informed Feghoot that they had elected a feminine President and Senate and a masculine Vice-President and House, that Absolute Equality was established, and that he must resign.

Feghoot himself arranged a great ceremony. With Senators and Representatives all on their perches, he presented the native President and Vice-President, who delivered splendid orations of welcome. When they had finished, however, the new Governess-General leaped to her feet in a fury. "Feghoot!" she cried. "Why were they using two speakers' stands? Why weren't they using the same one? It's discrimination! There's a misogynist in the House!"

"No, dear lady," said Ferdinand Feghoot. "They are trying to follow Earth customs. You told them time and again that on Earth we invariably have separate ladies' rostrums and gentlemen's rostrums."

In 2631, Ferdinand Feghoot found himself spaceship-wrecked on the fifth planet of Schimmelhorn III. The only other survivor was Dr. Jacqueline Cusp, the famous biologist, advocate of parthenogenesis, author of the popular work entitled *All Men Are Beasts*, and founder of a female movement which required its members to wear Mother Hubbards and full masks at all times.

In the wreck, their clothing had been almost completely burned off, but Feghoot, whose chivalry was proverbial, had salvaged part of the ship's cargo of cured hides at great risk to himself, and had fashioned robes for the two of them.

"We had no idea," he told his friend Robert Louis Stevenson on his next junket into the past, "that this planet was the home of the gnurrs, who devour fabrics, and leather, and even synthetics. That same night they descended upon us; and, without even disturbing us, ate up every one of the hides, including those we were wearing. At dawn I was wakened by the most hideous scream that ever I heard. The good doctor had found herself stark, staring naked!"

"It's an interesting story," commented Stevenson. "I might be able to use it if I could think of a title."

"Why not call it '*Dr. Jacqueline Missed Her Hide?*'" suggested Ferdinand Feghoot.

(with thanks to E. Nelson Bridwell)

FEGHOOT 38

On July 4th, 2007, Ferdinand Feghoot addressed the D.A.R.'s National Convention, hastily substituting for Robert A. Heinlein, who had been delayed on the Moon. Not knowing that his audience expected a more appropriate theme, he spoke on the many new nations of Africa.

"And in conclusion," he finally remarked, "I must mention the fascinating Republic of Gnus. We all know how, after the African bomb tests, the intelligence of the gnus suddenly rose to the human level, and how they organized and were admitted to the U.N. We know about their already great contributions to speculative philosophy and the arts of government. But few of us are aware of their tragedy—for the gnus soon learned that they have no aesthetic sense whatsoever. This made them feel deeply inferior. After years of searching, they shouted with joy when a young male showed signs of a singular genius for arranging glazed ceramic squares in pleasing patterns which were then made permanent with cement. They called me to examine this prodigy, and I gave him every imaginable test. But he was not truly talented. It was sadly indeed that I rendered my verdict—"

At this point, the President General leaned over to say that he should at least end his speech patriotically. "A simple slogan will suffice, dear Mr. Feghoot," she whispered.

"—Typical gnu and tiler too!" shouted Ferdinand Feghoot.

(with thanks to J.C. Owens)

In 3082, Ferdinand Feghoot married Gwendolyn Jane, Queen of New Camelot, and ruled there as King for a glorious fifty-five years.

Landing alone, he was seized by her varlets and hustled off to the Palace. Seeing at once that she was the most beautiful Queen in the galaxy, and that she wept pitifully, he asked what was wrong.

"Prithee, fair sir," she replied, "my knights all proposed marriage to me, and I refused every one. In anger, they took service with wicked King Borogrund, who makes war on me. Now I have only peasants. I can't arm them, for only knights can fight well. What will I d-d-do?" But when Feghoot suggested that she make them all knights, she sobbed that there wouldn't be time: the enemy would arrive in the hour.

Feghoot took action. Bringing electronic equipment, he jury-rigged a breadboard assembly, set it up in a tent, and had all her men file through. As each peasant emerged, his eyes flashed martial fire. Seizing axe, mace, or broadsword, he shouted, "Long live the Queen!"

King Borogrund's army was utterly shattered: only one wounded knight escaped to tell the sad tale. And the Queen, seating Feghoot beside her, said, "My Lord, they were perfectly splendid. Each man fought as though I had dubbed him myself! What did you do to them?"

"It's easy," answered Ferdinand Feghoot, "when you use printed sir kits."

(with thanks to Andrew Gould)

FEGHOOT 40

The Great Crisis of 1967 occurred when the vault at Fort Knox abruptly refused to come open. Experts of all sorts, including several notorious safecrackers borrowed from other Federal repositories, failed to budge it. As rumors leaked out, the subconscious feeling that there'd never really been anything there took hold, and even the Wall Street journal began to predict nationwide panic.

President Kennedy, still alert and decisive, at once phoned Ferdinand Feghoot, who was at a Science Fiction Convention in Bangkok; and when Ferdinand arrived at Fort Knox he found assembled the President, the Cabinet, the major dignitaries of the Executive, Legislative, and Judicial branches, and the Joint Chiefs of Staff. "We shall soon have it open, gentlemen," he said with a smile. "But first let's relax. Mr. President, may I suggest some sort of diversion—a game, shall we say?"

At once, the Chief Executive divided those present into two touch football teams, and appointed a Supreme Court justice as referee. But they had barely begun to play furiously when Feghoot stepped forward, seized the umpire's arm, and led him to the recalcitrant door. It flew open as soon as he touched it.

"How lucky it is," explained Ferdinand Feghoot, "that I prefer more sedentary games. Otherwise I might not have remembered that it almost always takes Jack's arbiter to open."

(with thanks to Herman W. Mudgett)

In 3964, Ferdinand Feghoot was summoned to Mikimoto, the world of intelligent pearls—round, glowing, crab-like creatures who spent the first part of their life cycle inside oysters. They had adopted English some centuries before, and were all highly cultured.

"Please assist us," begged their Queen. "We have lost Michael, our most eminent Doctor of Laws. He felt himself an outcast from birth, for his mother had committed our one unpardonable crime: she ran off with a sand crab. Poor Michael had a hideous disfigurement. He bore the marks of rutting in sand-beds—sand grains embedded all over him. In spite of his splendid career, it preyed on his mind. Yesterday, he jumped into the Vinegar Sea, our burial place and favorite spot for our suicides, since it slowly dissolves us away. We cannot enter it. Nor would we know how to find him among all the bodies."

Feghoot asked for directions, and departed at once. Within the hour he returned, bearing the chastened but now happy Michael, at last aware of the esteem and affection in which he was held.

"So soon!" cried the Queen. "How did you find him? Didn't the vinegar fumes fuddle your brain? How did you even remember?"

"Lustrous Lady," answered Ferdinand Feghoot, "as I waded through the Vinegar Sea in my sensitive bare feet, I just sang to myself, A gritty pearl is Michael, LL.D."

(with thanks to James L. Davidson)

It was Ferdinand Feghoot who, in 3234-zz-1877, saved the American Indian from cultural extinction. The learned Texarkana Uetbacq, Doctorette of Trans-temporal Sociology and Chairman of the Society for the Aesthetic Rearrangement of History, had decided that they must be totally integrated with the 19th Century post-Potato-Famine immigrant Irish.

"They are culturally sterile," she flatly declared. "No Indian ever invented anything."

At once, Feghoot challenged her to go back to 1877, and at once she accepted. On the Sioux Reservation, he escorted her to the teepee of the great Sitting Bull, who sat with vast dignity behind a fire of buffalo chips. His coup-sticks—bearing his scalps and other trophies of war—were fastened to a skin stretched overhead, something never previously seen.

"Ugh!" he announced. "Squaw look. Me great strategist. Me fix damfool Custer heap good. Huh—also fix Seventh Cavalry."

His visitor merely bristled.

"Ugh!" the old warrior went on, winking at Feghoot. "Also me great inventor. Me make heap good gadget first time."

"Rubbish!" sneered Miss Uetbacq. "You'll have to show me!"

"Ugh!" said Ferdinand Feghoot, pointing up at the trophies. "Squaw look—coup-stickal ceiling."

(with thanks to Joe Olson)

After Richard Wagner's visit to the planet Madamabutter-fry, where the natives claimed title to all operatic ideas and where he was summarily convicted on three counts of plagiarism,* he insisted that Ferdinand Feghoot take him back there directly. "It iss abzurd!" he shouted. "It iss they vhat are plachiarists. Mein ideas are mein own!"

Feghoot finally gave in; and on landing they were greeted by the very same police official who had arrested Wagner before. This time, the composer refused to be shown around. Marching into a suburban district, he entered a residence.

"Ha-ha!" he snorted, peering around. "Yott iss hier mit der idea for der opera?"

"There is this post, kindly sir," said the policeman, "which meets the above floor where is young girl's bedroom. In the night, her father puts only one rung in the hole of the post, so she can go up to bed. Then he takes it out to protect her."

He winked. "But sometimes a nice suitor is coming after papa makes sleep. So this girl takes a hammer from out of papa the tools chest, and puts in the hole of the post. Then she is hanging one garter upon to let the boy know he is welcome." He smiled at Wagner. "Therefore, goodly sir, you are under arrest."

"Dummkopft," screamed Wagner. "How could I shteal this idea for mein beaudtiful opera?"

"I'm afraid that it's only too obvious," replied Ferdinand Feghoot. "Gartered hammer-rung."

As explained in Feghoot 35. (with thanks to H. Orio Hoadley)

The mass migration of neo-beatniks from Earth to the Moon took place after 1980, when space travel became cheaper than staying at home. Soon beat bars were infringing on such luxurious developments as Moonolulu, Moon Goddess Meadows, and Sky-Vegas Executive Homes. Finally, after an all-night catnip-and-bhang party in the once sacrosanct lobby of the Copernicus-Hilton, the authorities took appropriate action. They summoned Ferdinand Feghoot from the 38th Century.

Feghoot timed in outside a beat hangout, "The Lunching Pad." It was surrounded by a menacing crowd of respectable citizens, uttering catcalls and brandishing golf clubs. The beat men, wearing huaraches, beards, tom jeans, and helmet liners decorated with abstract designs and Henry Miller quotations, beat their bongo-drums in the background. Their women were much more aggressive. Dressed in prolapsing black sweaters and leotards, they wore old nineteen-sixtyish hairdos which looked as though they had stood at just the wrong moment under very big birds, and which they had pulled out into hang-down scallops that almost covered their faces. They advanced, mouthing lewd threats, their ropy curtains thrust forward.

Obviously, only precisely the right phrase, instantly spoken could distract both sides and prevent civil war.

"Peekaboo, like!" chuckled Ferdinand Feghoot, pointing straight at the oncoming phalanx. "The Lunachick Fringe!"

FEGHOOT 45

On an excursion into Old Testament times, Ferdinand Feghoot became a close friend of the Prophet Ezekiel's and many were the long talks they had about morals, flying wheels, and the future of man.

So it was that Ezekiel revealed a vision unto him: "Lo! I was in what seemed a great valley of stone, and the walls thereof were carven into seats for a multitude, and the shape thereof was the shape of a diamond, with Angels at its four corners, and in the middle an Archangel, holding in his hand a hard ball. This he did throw with much force, and Angels with staves did strike at it to no avail; and so it continued for a period, and a second period, and five more, while the Archangel Gabriel did utter such mysteries as 'Strike three—that's Lucifer out!' and 'End of the seventh, still no score.' Then, on a sudden, all was changed. The Archangel Michael smote the ball so that it flew from the valley, and three other Angels who had reached the comers before him came running in; and the multitude beat their wings and shouted harmoniously, so that I was filled with great joy and awe. Then I turned, and saw that now the Lord's seat was empty, and sadness struck me that He was not there, and I have been depressed ever since."

Comfortingly, Feghoot patted the old gentleman's shoulder. "Don't worry about it, Ezekiel," he said. "Remember, in the big inning God created Heaven and Earth."

(with thanks to Peggy Kemerman)

In 3622, the ancient Bengali publishing firm of Mookerji, Dutt, & O'Toole sent Ferdinand Feghoot into the earliest periods of Indian history prospecting for bestseller material.

"Did you have any luck?" cried Pandit-Editor Bhupendranath Dutt on his return.

Feghoot smiled. "My friend, you know those legends about Krishna and the good time he had with the milkmaids? They're true! I got there on his seventeenth birthday. He welcomed me to his staff. It was just like the pictures, except that the parties were held in a really magnificent cow barn—a regular palace—not out in the open." He sighed. "Believe me, they don't make women like that any more."

"Splendid!" Dutt shouted. "We'll sell millions of copies! And subsidiary rights! And American sales! And—" His face fell abruptly. "Dear me, dear me. We can't do it. It would be sacrilegious. Even the adolescent Lord Krishna is much too exalted. It could never sell here as nonfiction. But—but perhaps you could make it a novel? That's it!" He rubbed his hands with relief. "Of course, it would have to have a good title—one redolent with the fragrant breath of the Orient, of the Mysterious East."

"I know," said Ferdinand Feghoot. I'm going to call it *The Moo-House of the August Teen.*"

The humans of Onderdonck III were decidedly decadent. The felines, on the contrary, had mutated and progressed very rapidly. When Ferdinand Feghoot arrived there, in 3708, cats had almost all the good jobs, especially in Government service, and relations between the two species were decidedly strained.

At this juncture, a young chap named Thomas Meowwr-reow was arrested for causing the death of a human called Petrus V. Parsnipp, a pioneer balloonist. Another human, Abercorn Sludge, had allegedly paid him to loosen the cords holding the ballast to Parsnipp's balloon, thereby causing it "to soar rapidly, to become covered with ice, and to crash with fatal results to the aeronaut."

Defense attorneys on Onderdonck III had to share the punishment of the accused if convicted, so poor Thomas could find no one to aid him. Only extreme verbal brilliance, the lawyers all knew, could dazzle a jury enough to procure an acquittal, and they despaired of their talents.

But Feghoot came forward. In court, he laughed at the seemingly overwhelming evidence marshaled by the Prosecutor. Then he spoke the great sentence which won the case instantly.

"It is well-known," declared Ferdinand Feghoot, "that Tom untied weight for no man."

(with thanks to . . . ?)

In 1962, the heads of three major TV networks begged Ferdinand Feghoot to advise them. "Freedom of speech is at stake!" cried A. Cerberus Mishmash. "Besides, we all shall lose money! It's that man Norman Minow! He's forced me to cancel Rape West of the Pecos—a nice, clean, family show, no nakedness in it!"

"That's right," put in one of his fellows, "and we had to scrap Sadist after lining up seven sponsors. Don't American children have any rights anymore?"

"You know what he called us?" shouted the other. "It was in this morning's Drew Pearson. Abominable Snowmen—and Hillary proved they don't even exist!"

"Feghoot," Mishmash demanded, "how long must we put up with him? Will he hold office for decades, like J. Edgar Hoover?" He shuddered. "Or is this only a phase? You know the future; you can tell us. It's worth sixty-four thousand—maybe more."

"It won't last very long," Feghoot replied with a smile.

There were three sighs of relief. "That's fine," crowed Mishmash, as he wrote out the check. "Say, won't it be good to get back in the groove!"

"Oh, you won't be able to do that," said Ferdinand Feghoot. "Your industry will never be quite the same again. You see, it's now passing through what we can only describe as its Minow-pause."

It would be a mistake to assume that none of Ferdinand Feghoot's many contributions to Literature were on a popular level. His Trans-Temporal Fellowships in Creative Writing were especially designed to improve the quality of the so-called historical novel. They were a form of shock therapy; prolific popular writers, hypnotized into secrecy, were shown important events not only in the colorful past but also in the even more colorful future.

Thus, he once took a well-known mid-Twentieth Century American writer to witness the mass conversion of the Agha Khan and his followers by the Bishop of Exeter in 2112. The Bishop, a close friend of his, provided the writer a seat from which he could see every detail of the solemn ceremony, including its dramatic culmination, when the Agha Khan and his wife (an Italian actress of really splendid proportions) both knelt to kiss the Episcopal ring.

"I've never been so—well, impressed," he told the Bishop afterwards in the vestry. "No one could have made me believe that the spiritual head of a whole Moslem sect would get down on one knee to submit to the incumbent of an Anglican Bishopric! But—but what use can I make of it? I mean, in my career?"

"Why, it'll inspire your most popular work," said Ferdinand Feghoot. "Just imagine—*The Agha Knee and the Exeter See.*"

By 2399, the reborn Venetian Republic again ruled the commerce of the Mediterranean, and its Citizens were known as the sharpest of traders. But they couldn't cheat Ferdinand Feghoot.

"H-here is our problem, Signor," wept the Doge, as his gilded State Barge drew up to the Piazza San Marco. "Once, our most famous tourist attraction! And now—we cannot see even the stones, the lions, the horses!" Opening his umbrella, he clambered ashore. "All over—pigeons! You must drive them away! We pay a million in gold! Look, a recorder—we set down the contract at once."

Feghoot agreed. Within the hour, his technicians were in the piazza. They had mechanical weasels with a metallic fur that shrilled hideously when they moved, and robot owls which ceaselessly uttered the ominous cry of their prototype.

The pigeons became quite hysterical. They took off directly, flew to Algiers, and never returned. But when Feghoot asked for his pay, the Doge smiled cynically. "Signor, you stipulated that you would get rid of the pigeons—but it was done instead by the sound of mechanical weasels and owls. We owe you nothing at all!"

Feghoot switched on the playback. "Listen carefully," he chuckled. "I voiced the contract myself. It says very distinctly, 'The pigeons will be driven away by fur din and fake hoot.'"

(with thanks to John F. Moore)

Ferdinand Feghoot not only shared the hardships of General Washington's soldiers at Valley Forge, but he managed to protect his fellow Time Watcher, Coop-Major Leghorn Gallinorum, from their hunger. Feghoot was disguised as a volunteer Neapolitan officer; the Coop-Major, a telepathic mutant rooster from the 43rd Century, as a gamecock. They were watching for a British sympathizer who, along that time-line, was due to make an attempt on Washington's life.

Finally, late in February, Baron von Steuben summoned Feghoot excitedly. "Ach!" he cried out. "In der bones I haff der stranche feeling—Vashington iss in danger!"

Responding immediately, Feghoot's colleague began searching the area where the Baron felt especially uneasy, and very promptly he discovered the culprit, cunningly hidden in an old cider press.

When the man had been led off to court-martial, they settled down to their evening meal of boiled boot tops and birchbark; and von Steuben, looking hungrily at the Coop-Major and licking his chops, sighed that there was nothing he missed as much as old-fashioned Italian cooking. "Donnerwetter!" he exclaimed. "I vould giff anything for pollo al burro, pollo con funghi, for chust plain pollo!"

"My dear Baron," laughed Ferdinand Feghoot. "Have you forgotten your calories, your cholesterol? Don't you realize that you just had a first-rate chicken catch a Tory?"

(with thanks to Robert E. Spenger)

FEGHOOT 52

It was Ferdinand Feghoot who, in 2839, averted the greatest fraud in all history. The twin worlds of Gyppo and Pigeon Drop had the highest mutation rate ever known. Their inhabitants provided freaks for the galaxy's sideshows, and specialized in revolting "wild man" acts, swallowing live hair-slugs from Lovecraft 14, and biting the heads off wet, wriggling slurbwinders. They were notorious for their rigged games and elaborate confidence tricks.

Then they abruptly "reformed." They joined respectable churches, confessed every detail of their past swindles, and impressed everyone with their fervor. Soon ministers were giving them character references; bankers and lawyers were co-signing their notes.

Feghoot remained unconvinced. Though reviled and ridiculed by the popular press, he pushed his campaign for a thorough investigation by the Galactic Intelligence Agency to a successful conclusion, and the results proved how right he was. The Gypponians and Pigeon Droppers had planned to salt their deserts with priceless gaborium, to sell mining stock everywhere, and then to evade prosecution by taking advantage of an obscure immunity clause in the Grand Charter.

"Tell me, how on earth did you know it?" asked the President-General, as he hung the supreme decoration around Feghoot's neck.

"It was obvious, sir," answered Ferdinand Feghoot. "'Beware of geeks baring grifts.'"

(with thanks to W. Robert Gibson)

The Society for the Aesthetic Rearrangement of History would ordinarily never have thought of sending Ferdinand Feghoot on a mission to maintain the historical status quo.

However, one such occasion arose when James Watt, whose destiny it had been to perfect (if not invent) the steam engine, seemed sure to succeed in the competitive examinations for a clerk's post at the Royal Observatory.

"You must go back and stop him!" shouted Dr. Corydon Bramahpootra, the Society's President. "This lovely Gibbonian period of history is Classically perfect. We must keep it intact!"

In Watt's time, the Observatory's main concern was to provide mariners with accurate astronomical data, and a knowledge of navigation was of prime importance. Feghoot cleverly engineered his own election to the Examination Board, and as one of the questions he put in the following problem: "You are at the Straits of Gibraltar, bound for Ragusa. What course would you set and how long would you hold it?"

Then he provided Watt with a specially distorted chart, and awaited results. As he had planned, when Watt's paper was being corrected, it turned out that the course he had given would have taken him to the Equator at about longitude 32°.

At once, Ferdinand Feghoot rejected him as a candidate, and on the paper he wrote his reason for so doing: "Watt's course for Ragusa's a course for Uganda."

(with thanks to John K.H. Brunner)

It was not often that Ferdinand Feghoot was mistaken in matters of interplanetary business. Once, however, in 2073, his advice was requested by a Mrs. Klipspringer, a famous breeder of pedigreed dogs who lived in a small town in Connecticut. So successful had she been that she was planning to extend her operations to other planets.

Feghoot considered very carefully, and finally informed her that no bank in the universe would lend her the necessary capital.

"Then I shall go to old Silas Quibble, the money lender right back in my home town!" she flared.

Quibble was a notoriously tough customer; and Feghoot, with a smile, asked what she proposed to put up as collateral.

"My favorite dog," she angrily answered, "Triple Galactic Champion Fu Chu of Chow Yuk!"

Feghoot coldly informed her that she would be wasting her time, and ushered her out.

The very next day, she came back in triumph, waving Silas Quibble's certified check. "He advanced every cent of it," she exulted, "and a few thousand more!"

Ferdinand Feghoot leaped to his feet in astonishment. "I stand amazed!" he cried out. "Silent upon a Peke in Darien!"

(with thanks to Ruth S. Perot)

The beautiful but psychotic Cleopatra II ascended the restored throne of Egypt in 2054. She at once set about revising society according to the notions of her favorite novelist, Aldous Huxley. She had every Egyptian classified from Alpha to Epsilon, with set duties and drudgeries. She ordered all children into State nurseries to be properly conditioned. She decreed sexual promiscuity.

Chaos ensued, and her desperate Ministers finally called in Ferdinand Feghoot, who warned them that her case was so far advanced that even he could only guarantee to arrest it.

Disguised as one of her lovers, Feghoot embraced the Queen passionately, gave her a tranquilizer, put her under hypnosis, and in three weeks of expert psychotherapy effected what seemed a full cure. The Queen rescinded all her decrees and submitted to Constitutional government. She showered Feghoot with honors and jewels.

A month later, however, in the Times, he saw the brief headline Repentant Queen Paints Dam Gray. The story stated that Cleopatra II had caused the great Aswan Dam to be painted with 4000 tons of deep-penetrating gray cement stain. "It will stand as a perpetual reminder of my folly," she was quoted as saying.

"It is as I feared," sighed Ferdinand Feghoot. "The cure is not complete. Failing to create a brave new world, the Queen after mania somber dyes Aswan."

(with thanks to Cora Anne Cunningham)

The natives of Qsgg III, besides being exceedingly vain of their sciences and arts, were the busiest non-humanoids in the galaxy. In their desire to excel, they produced new theories and gadgets by the hundreds of thousands, created astounding new architectures, made mobiles, painted, and composed concerti from morning to night. Only in the performing arts were they really inferior, and they struggled for years to perfect electronic musical instruments which would function properly in their highly charged atmosphere. Finally, in 2992, they announced their success, boasting of a conductor's baton which automatically controlled all charged atoms.

It was Ferdinand Feghoot, the most honest, perceptive, and sensitive of all critics, whom they asked to be the sole judge at the premiere. The program consisted of "El Amor Brujo," "Nights in the Gardens of Spain," "La Vida Breve," and all of "The Three-Cornered Hat."

Feghoot listened attentively to the quite splendid performance, and it was some time before he sadly delivered his verdict—that they had failed to surpass the greatest musicians of Earth.

They were stricken. Heaping urq on their nz', they burst into the shrill pentatonic wail which was their form of weeping.

"Please, please," begged Ferdinand Feghoot, touched to the core. "Please don't take on so! Believe me, it's not any lack of ability. You've just got too many ions in de Falla!"

(with thanks to Hugh Franklin)

FEGHOOT 57

The intelligent amphibious Eels of Proxima Centauri XIII were found by Ferdinand Feghoot during the Space Race—to the annoyance of the Russians, whose expedition showed up only after the Eels had learned English and were trading away with the West.

The Eels were ruled by Great Mother Eel, and their well-being depended on how happy she was. Singing, dancing, telling tales, they all did their best to amuse her. The Russians, seeing this, decided to bore from within. Their agents were disguised as encyclopedia salesmen, progressive educators, and TV comedians—and were almost as boring. Before long, Mother Eel became tired and fidgety and unpleasant. Soon there was social unrest everywhere.

Feghoot returned swiftly from Earth. He brought a book full of funny old jokes, all based on the quaint speech of Irishmen, Southerners, Swedes, and whatever. Mother Eel had never heard anything like them before. Making him read them over and over again, she laughed till she quivered. She really was tickled. Her subjects rejoiced; perfect harmony was restored.

The Russian commander was furious. His patrols kidnapped Feghoot in space. "Exploiter of class-conscious Eels!" he bellowed. "You have spoiled my wonderful boring! Maybe soon I am liquidated!"

"But, Comrade," protested Ferdinand Feghoot. "Have I not converted them to Dialect-Tickle-Mater-Eel-ism?"

(with thanks to Mrs. Jules J. Perot)

Ferdinand Feghoot was the first man to follow Burton's Time Track back into the other-real world of the Arabian Nights Entertainments and sail with Sindbad the Sailor.

Sindbad, just promoted Grand Admiral, would take no advice. Though Feghoot argued for more practical projects, like a search after roes' eggs, he insisted that a vessel propelled by genii in bottles could circumnavigate the Rim of the World without falling off, and he succeeded in convincing the Sultan.

Hardly had they cleared the Bab el Mandeb when a storm overtook them, the greatest that ever was seen. The ship sprung a leak. The genii flew off en masse. And Sindbad and Feghoot alone survived to reach an unknown island inhabited only by lean wild asses.

"I have heard that wild asses can be baked into savory pies," said Sindbad dejectedly.

On this diet they lived eighteen months. When they finally were rescued, Feghoot—the greatest of gourmets—preferred charges at once, so successfully that the Sultan passed sentence without further ado, demoting Sindbad to Seaman Third-Class.

"Protector of the Poor!" screamed Sindbad. "I am being punished only for wishing to serve you—for my soaring ambition!"

"On the contrary," murmured Ferdinand Feghoot. "You are being punished for my wild ass pie rations."

(with thanks to G. O. Guntharp, Jr.)

Like George Washington, Ferdinand Feghoot could not tell a lie. This was dramatically demonstrated in 2362, when he rescued Magda Millsap-Borgia, most famous and beautiful of operatic sopranos, from the clutches of Adrian Haggis, an infamous booking agent who, through illegal time-traveling connections, kidnapped great female voices from the past and the future. Because of him, the Twentieth Century was renowned for having more super-sopranos than any other period in history.

Luckily, Magda was snatched from her dressing room in the vast Pinole Opera House just before she was to receive the coveted Tony, an award like the Oscar of pioneer days. Feghoot, who was supposed to present it, set off in instant pursuit, but Haggis hid her so cunningly that a full week went by in her world before her return. The news media had a regular field day—she had eloped with a Martian! she had eloped with her husband! she was having an affair with Ferdinand Feghoot, who also was missing! When she came back, it was all Feghoot could do to pacify the reporters.

"You managed them ever so nicely," she told him at supper that evening. "But—naughty boy!—why did you say I'd been held captive in the mountains of California? Ooh, what a fib!"

"My dear," replied Ferdinand Feghoot, "I told them only the absolute truth. I said I had rescued you from the High C Era."

In the 28th Century, Ferdinand Feghoot always took passage on spaceships from Argol. Their discipline was rigidly based on Terran naval tradition. Indeed, Argolian law compelled every captain, on assuming command, to identify himself absolutely with some sea-going hero of Earth, actual or legendary. One wore an eye-patch, another a false wooden leg; some carried harpoons, spyglasses, or belaying pins; they wore pea-jackets or gold-braided coats, and uttered such phrases as "Yo-ho-ho!" and "Damn the torpedoes!"

On the trip to Argol itself, Feghoot met a young captain whose only peculiarity was his habit of sounding the ship's klaxon several times whenever they made planetfall. He explained that he was warning his crew of temptations aground—as many blasts of the klaxon as there were loose women per thousand of population. Feghoot approved, and was shocked when the captain, on arrival at Argol, was placed under arrest for having no Terran prototype. Gladly undertaking his defense, he explained to the Court about the temptation index and warning.

"And what," sneered the Prosecuting Officer, "has all this to do with the great heroes of Terran seas? Nothing whatever!"

"You are wrong," replied Ferdinand Feghoot. "Throughout your whole fleet this splendid young man is known as Captain Horatio Hornblower!"

(with thanks to John F. Moore)

Of Ferdinand Feghoot's contributions to English literature none were more important than those in the field of fantasy. He often took promising writers on trips to the future, to far planets, or along strange time-tracks into worlds of What-If. But the drug yald he reserved for the most talented, and it was seldom indeed that he took anyone to its brewing place.

But in the mid-1930s, he went there, escorting a young British philologist. "Yald will open your Eye-Into-Wonder," he said, as the Cup floated in. "Drink it, and look at the Place Where There Should Be A Prism."

The Englishman hesitated.

"Don't worry," said Feghoot, "it's perfectly harmless. Now—down the hatch!" Then he left the cave quietly.

Scarcely ten minutes later, he was summoned back by a cry of great agitation. "Mr. Feghoot!" the alarmed writer exclaimed. "Look—there's a being! He—he's only four feet tall, with red cheeks, and a brass-buttoned coat, and—and short breeches. And his feet are all furry! He's telling me the most wonderful story. But—but he's an hallucination. He simply took shape there! And you told me the drug would do me no harm!"

"My dear Tolkien," said Ferdinand Feghoot. "I said it was harmless. I never said it was non-Hobbit-forming."

In 1989, Ferdinand Feghoot's assistance was desperately called for by the most independent and powerful of all great corporations, the Universal Telephone and Telegraph Company.

"Mr. Feghoot," pleaded its distraught emissary, "nothing works right any more. Our communications satellites, our Earthside transmitters, even the sets in our copters and cars haven't worked since last Tuesday. As soon as you switch them on they give out one deep, bell-like note—and that's all! It's driving us crazy. I'm so worried that I can't remember whether my own number is 3502-472296-859-00067-33 or 2503-742926-589-06007-88 or—" He began sobbing pitifully.

"Have you no clue to the cause?" Feghoot asked.

"W-we know what it is. It's a ray from the s-s-system of Altair. It was turned on on Tuesday, and we've had n-n-nothing but those awful bell-like notes ever since! It's an Altarian plot, Mr. Feghoot! Please, please help us."

"Now, now, Mr. Coupling," soothed Ferdinand Feghoot. "It's no plot, really it isn't. This just happens to be one of those rays when everything goes Dong!"

(with thanks to Vee Heintzelman)

In 3945, Ferdinand Feghoot invented his Para-Time Traveller, which enabled him to visit legendary and mythological figures in those eras when they might have existed.

He immediately sought out Paul Bunyan, whom he found in the middle para-1800s, busily logging off and draining the Great Dakota Swamp. "Say, am I glad to see you!" boomed Bunyan. "I got a problem, and I know you can help me. But first I'll show you around." They spent the rest of the day inspecting the vast logging camp, and ended up at the gigantic combined bunk house and inn Paul had built at the edge of the marsh for his men and hordes of tourists who flooded there. Proudly, he displayed his ingenious system of conduits for pressurizing the upper stories, the mile-wide sheet of metal he used as a frying pan, and his gravy vats—each over a hundred yards in diameter.

"And right there's my problem," he announced gloomily, pointing at thousands of strange stick-like creatures flitting over the vats. "I had to figure out how to keep stirring the gravy so's to keep it from burning, so I crossed canoe paddles with dragonflies and trained the young 'uns to fly like you see. Now everyone wants to know what I call 'em and I just can't think of a name folks'll remember. Feghoot, can you?"

"Marsh In Flying Sauce Oars," said Ferdinand Feghoot.

(with thanks to Richard Olcott)

The singular gravitational field of Hennypenny's Planet made it perfect for the raising of poultry. The Northern Hemisphere, where gravity was only at Moon level, was ideal for breasts, thighs, and drumsticks; the Southern, where it was three times Earth's, produced unequaled egg crops. Consequently the entire population was prosperous, and millions of retired librarians, sea captains, and mathematics professors made fortunes almost without lifting a finger.

But there was one fly in their ointment. Their hilly world had only short-distance radio, and their technology was inadequate to the problem. Naturally, they called in Ferdinand Feghoot—and in a very few days he had long-range transmissions going full blast.

"Mr. Feghoot," cried the Elders, as they measured him for his statue, "how did you do it? And at such a low cost?"

"It wasn't too hard," their benefactor replied modestly. "What you lacked was something to reflect radio waves back to the surface, so I simply took one of your wonderful Southern Hemisphere hens and placed her in orbit."

"But—but we don't understand. How could one of our very own hens—?"

"Look at it this way," said Ferdinand Feghoot. "I provided your planet with a heavy side layer."

(with thanks to Simon Kahn)

In 2856, the Members of the newly formed Time-Travellers Club sent Ferdinand Feghoot off to investigate the hazards they might expect to encounter in the pursuit of their hobby.

"Now take care," warned Dame Electra MacClinch, the Club's first Temporary President. "Try not to get lost, and be sure to get back here promptly next Thursday."

The Members gave Feghoot three rousing cheers; and, stepping through the)(in the wall, he immediately vanished.

When he returned, after seventeen years, his reception was very much colder. Alerted by the time shuttle's signal, the Membership had assembled, and Dame Electra was regarding him with a frosty gray eye.

He was wearing a kilt, and he had Robert Burns with him. Each had an arm round a pretty but slightly overripe woman in the dress of the late 18th Century, and they had obviously been having a wonderful time.

Feghoot introduced the great poet; then with a chuckle he presented Nell Trott and Meg Lively.

"I have heard of this Burns person," sniffed Dame Electra. "But what are these—creatures?"

"Hoot, lass—they're famous!" laughed Ferdinand Feghoot. "Hae ye no heard o' the pair o' doxies of time travel?"

(with thanks to Romina Grobis)

When the Super-Viking, Poul Mohandasson, established the Indo-Danish Imperium in 5107, he at once made Ferdinand Feghoot his Grand Helmsman. Then, from his Throne—which showed the wedding of Wotan and Devi in the frankest possible detail—he ordered all nations to sign an agreement never to take part in wars of the Galaxy.

"Ho-ho!" he boomed. "So I cover up my space-raiding! See to it! A tremendous occasion—all aliens must be deceived!"

Feghoot set about organizing the affair. Treasuries were looted to pay for luxuriant new gardens on the Malabar Coast. Earth's fairest maidens were summoned, famous scientists, saddhus and swamis, the Heads of State and diplomats of all known worlds. Newsmen and telecasters arrived by the thousands. Then the gardens were ringed by hard-bitten troops, splendidly uniformed, with secret instructions.

Finally the great day arrived. The Super-Viking himself entered, wearing his horned Turban of State. He took one look, leaped from his howdah, and bellowed, "Ferdinand Grendelson, what have you done? They've all been stripped naked!"

He seized his huge drinking horn, took a comforting draught—and spat it out instantly. "ORANGE PEKOE!" he roared.

"Everyone's drinking it, Most Rapacious High Admiral," said Ferdinand Feghoot. "It'll be a sensation. For the first time in history, the whole world will sign a nude rally tea pact."

(with thanks to E. Nelson Bridwell)

TEA?!

It was against Ferdinand Feghoot's advice that Ezra P. Crosshatch, Member of the Time-Travellers Club and well-known poet, decided to take a Massachusetts vacation during the 17th Century.

"Ah, Feghoot," he cried, "not for me are the suave sins of Byzantium, the sophistications of Second-Empire Paris, the machine-made wickedness of Las Vegas! My soul wants simplicity!"

Feghoot knew that Crosshatch had recently spent his New Fulbright with Henry Thoreau wading around Walden Pond, and that he was still under the influence. Therefore, he said nothing more. But he was in no way surprised when the poet failed to come back on schedule and the alarm light went on.

As Chairman of the Club's Rescue Committee, Feghoot at once sped back to Salem 1667, where he found Crosshatch exposed in the public pillory. Eggs which urchins had thrown at him stained his clothing, and he looked very unhappy. Sullenly he explained that he had been caught pinching a milkmaid.

"You ought to have warned me," he whined, as Feghoot unfastened his hands. "You never said it would be as awful as this."

"I made myself perfectly clear," replied Ferdinand Feghoot. "I told you you'd find yourself in a simple old two-wrist trap."

As a Jurist, Ferdinand Feghoot made his great reputation largely on Pigafetta's Planet, adjudicating the complex insurance cases which arose from the nature and habits of its inhabitants, who were merfolk. Especially celebrated was his decision when the most beautiful mermaid of all, the actress Dolphina, tried to collect several million for a pregnancy which she said was an accident.

Arranging herself on the stand so that photographers would have a chance to get plenty of what, on her world, was called "fishcake," she smiled winningly up at Feghoot.

"Dolphina, my dear," her lawyer began, "did you have any—hm-mmm—relations with mermen during the period involved?"

Blushing prettily, she replied that she hadn't.

"How about Earthmen?" he asked.

"Certainly not."

Innumerable witnesses supported this statement, adding that she hadn't so much as been seen with a man, and her attorney dramatically rested his case, stating that the lack of opportunity proved her case absolutely.

"Not at all," ruled Ferdinand Feghoot. "You have shown conclusively that the plaintiff consorted with neither mermen nor men. But this does not prove that her pregnancy was an accident. On the contrary, I am forced to attribute it to an active cod."

When wed in 3000 A.D.
Feghoot flouted tradition's decree
    That a smoked salmon's head
    lie in each nuptial bed—
"For love laughs at lox myths," said he.

(with thanks to Simon Kahn)

Ferdinand Feghoot was an ardent admirer of the great Sarah Bernhardt. It was whispered in Paris that he would do anything for her.

One cold winter day in the 1870s, they were strolling together along the Left Bank when suddenly, right before them, an elderly gentleman threw up his hands, cried out, "Adieu! All is lost!" and cast himself into the river.

"Helas, it is Aristide Plonc, the good landlord!" screamed la Bernhardt. "Aristide, try to swim! Come in to the bank! Look, I will hold out my parasol to you!"

"I refuse!" cried the old man. "I am bankrupt! None of my tenants have paid me! I will not come in!" And he went under again.

At that point, Feghoot took off his coat, plunged into the chill waters, and effected the rescue. After they had taken M. Plonc home, dried him, filled him with cognac, and paid his most pressing bills, Sarah embraced Feghoot warmly.

"You are brave, mon ami," she purred in his ear. "Poor Aristide, why did he do it? He must have been out of his mind!"

"Oh no," replied Ferdinand Feghoot. "He just didn't have enough rents to come in out of the Seine."

It was Ferdinand Feghoot who, in Homeric times, first raised the Oracle of Delphi to full prominence. Its Pythoness and its Holy Ones had been scurvily treated and worse paid by the Greek rulers who were beginning to seek advice there. The sensitive Pythoness was above such mundane matters as money, and the Holy Ones were the world's worst administrators. They agreed to put their financial affairs and public relations into Feghoot's competent hands, and he speedily organized them into the PHOU, the Pan-Hellenic Oracular Union.

Their next customers, an assortment of Tyrants, Kings, Autarchs, and Obligarchs from some twenty Greek cities, were presented a very stiff schedule of rates which, tremendously angered, they refused absolutely to pay. For weeks, they camped at the Oracle, bitterly denouncing Feghootes the Barbarian.

Finally, Feghoot gave them his ultimatum. "If you refuse to pay up," he said, "we'll leave Greece bag and baggage and go over to Asia Minor. Then who'll answer your questions?"

"NEVER!" roared a Spartan, shaking his spear. "It would be revolution! It would be rebellion against all the gods!"

"Nonsense!" replied Ferdinand Feghoot. "It'll just be a sybil rites movement."

By 2322, all Africa was divided into three Empires, those of the Black Muslims, the Black Mormons, and the Black Masons, all engaged in the most intense cultural rivalry.

Ludwig Bifuwayo, who as Thrice-Exalted Supreme Noble Grand exercised absolute power in the Masonic domain, was especially anxious to outshine the others. One day, in distress, he called Ferdinand Feghoot. "Mr. Feghoot," he moaned, "it's about my son Jack. Eventually he'll inherit my throne. His education and culture must excel those of all rival rulers. I have imported the greatest of scholars, the rarest of books. I have sought the most eminent witchdoctors, the most costly psychiatrists. I have given the lad every advantage. I have allowed him to keep a pet anteater. I have even flown in an entire theatrical troupe from Kyoto to amuse him." His voice broke. "B-but he—he just seems to take less and less interest, to get m-more and more stupid."

To his utter astonishment, Feghoot grinned cheerfully.

"You m-m-mock me," wept the ruler.

"Certainly not, Your Magnificence," declared Ferdinand Feghoot. "It's just that you yourself gave me the answer. Take the anteater away! Send the troupe back to Nippon! Aardvark and Noh Play make Jack a dull boy."

On all five planets of the Anchovian System (Anchovy I, Anchovy II, Anchovy III, Goats' Heaven, and Egg), ghosts were perfectly visible, mingling freely with their live friends and relations. But only on Anchovy III were the spirits of living inhabitants as easily perceived. The natives were so proud of this fact that they snubbed everyone else in the Galaxy, refusing even to exchange ambassadors until Ferdinand Feghoot convinced them that their uniqueness was entirely illusory.

"We don't wave our souls around out in public," he told them, "but that doesn't mean we can't see them ourselves. And they aren't simple geometrical shapes like your own. Why, even our animals all have souls pleasantly shaped like letters of the alphabet. Come to Earth with me. Even if you won't believe what I tell you, surely you'll trust this innocent child." He introduced his son, Ferdinand Junior, then seven years old.

Sneering, the Anchovians accepted. Once on Earth, Feghoot took them for a walk in the country, where presently, in a meadow, they saw a sway-backed old nag, looking dismal.

"Well?" they demanded.

"That's a D-spirited horse," piped little Ferdinand.

The envoys grumbled unpleasantly and trudged on. Then, from a tree, they heard a large bird going, Hoo! Hoo! Hoo!

"Look, Papa!" cried the boy, before they could ask. "There's a Y-souled owl!"

The Anchovians were furious. Their spirits began to glow luridly. At that instant, a fuzzy caterpillar appeared before them, and one of them at once ground the poor creature into the path with his huge mottled foot.

"L-l-look what you've done!" shrilled the lad, starting to cry. "You've rubbed him right out!"

"So okay!" growled the Anchovian. "So describe me the soul."

"H-h-he was E-wraithed," lisped Ferdinand Junior.

Feghoot's son Garthwaite, a six year old, wet his bed every night, to the great distress of his parents. Every remedy was exhausted: physicians, psychiatrists, hypnotists. Finally, Feghoot himself contrived an ingenious device which, at the very first sign of the accident happening, set off an alarm bell.

It worked to perfection. So swift and shrill was it that Garthwaite was always awakened in time to avoid all but the tiniest dampness. Night after night, this occurred, and the boy began to get sulky and fretful. "That silly old bell!" he complained. "It wakes me up all the time. I'd sooner be wet."

"Don't worry, son," his father assured him. "Pretty soon you won't need it at all."

Sure enough a night came when the bell didn't ring—but the accident happened. Feghoot soon learned the truth of it.

The precocious child, having cleverly short-circuited the alarm, was looking very smug about the whole business.

At once, frowning terribly, he turned him over his knee.

"Daddy!" screamed Garthwaite. "Y-y-you aren't going to g-give me a spanking?"

"What did you expect me to give you?" roared Ferdinand Feghoot. "A new Nobel Peace Prize?"

Ferdinand Feghoot was the confidant of Nicolas Restif de la Bretonne, the French 18th Century pornographer; and it was to Feghoot alone that Restif divulged his most closely held secret—the strange English branch of his family in Buckinghamshire.

Feghoot naturally wanted to meet them.

"No, no, dear friend!" Restif exclaimed. "They strike terror into everyone's heart! Imagine, they were even expelled from the unspeakable Hell-Fire Club! Were it not for Uncle Nathaniel, I shudder to think what might happen. His will is of iron. Only he can control them."

But Feghoot prevailed, and a week later they approached Direwolf Hall. A wicked darkness had fallen.

"Oh, I do hope Uncle Nathaniel hasn't gone up to London!" moaned Restif as sounds of ungodly revelry reached their ears.

At that instant, a half-naked wench dashed into the road screaming horribly; two burly men burst into view fighting with daggers; and a terrified clergyman came running toward them.

"Gentlemen, go no further, I pray you!" he cried. "Hell has opened! Satan and all his imps are abroad!"

"Calm yourself, Reverend Sir," said Ferdinand Feghoot, quite unperturbed. "It isn't as bad as all that. The Restifs are Nateless tonight."

By making sure that Columbus discovered America, Ferdinand Feghoot earned the undying respect of Queen Isabella and did more than anyone else to temper the cruelties of the Inquisition.

As Fernando al-Feghut, a converted moor, he soon became Soothsayer in Ordinary to the Queen, who was being swayed by two factions, and he speedily saw that the key to the problem lay in her recognizing Columbus' importance when he showed up. However, the strict rules of the Society for the Aesthetic Rearrangement of History forbade him to tell her directly.

One day the Queen summoned him secretly. "What shall I do, Learned Sir?" said she. "Shall I just roast some more heretics? Or shall I send fleets out to sea after conquest and treasure? Pray gaze in your great crystal ball and inform me."

Obediently, Feghoot gazed. "Your Majesty, an Admiral will come! He will sail abroad to your vast profit and power!"

"But, Señor, how shall I know him?"

Again Feghoot stared. "I see a hand!" he declared. "It holds a vial of a light, clear fluid, divinely perfumed. Behold! Lovely ladies dab it here and there, anoint themselves with it!"

"Dare you speak riddles to me, insolent Moor?" stormed Isabella. "What means this?"

"Crystal Ball Cologne," said Ferdinand Feghoot.

FEGHOOT 77

On the planet Greenthumb, the flowers of Earth not only burgeoned but mutated fantastically. In fifty years, they were mobile; in a hundred, intelligent. Soon they formed social structures like man's—marrying, having love affairs, raising their offspring, fighting their neighbors.

Finally, out of nowhere, a Leader appeared who threatened all institutions, human and vegetable.

Ferdinand Feghoot was asked to investigate and offer a remedy. Presently he reported: "Some years ago, an especially lovely young flower—indeed, she was Miss Greenthumb of 3887—was seduced by a handsome, unscrupulous male begonia, intrigued by the slight difference between his species and hers. She abandoned the unfortunate fruit of this union, who had to live by his wits, pilfering fertilizer, putting down roots wherever he could. He grew up embittered. Today, he swears he'll rule the whole planet as absolute dictator."

"What can we do?" cried people and flowers alike. "How can we stop him?"

"You cannot," said Ferdinand Feghoot. "Don't you see? This is no common conqueror. You cannot resist—this is the Waif of the Fuchsia!"

Antique collecting flourished as never before during the Greater East Asia Popular Democratic Co-Prosperity (or Mitsubishi) Shogunate. The greatest collector of all was the twenty-ninth Shogun, Pedro Miguel Masayoshi IV, who enforced honesty among dealers with admirable strictness, elevating those who told the strict truth to samurai rank and decapitating any who didn't.

On one occasion, he purchased a charming Sung Dynasty statuette of Avalokitesvara, the Boddhisatva commonly called the Goddess of Mercy, from a respectable dealer named Anastasio Yamada, a friend of Ferdinand Feghoot's. After assuring him in good faith of its genuineness, poor Yamada discovered that it was a fake. In distress, he told Feghoot the story. "If I lie to the Shogun," he moaned, "I and my ancestors will suffer disgrace. If now I tell him the truth, he will cut off my head! Feghoot-sama, what shall I do?"

"Never fear," Feghoot assured him. "I shall attend to it."

"I know he'll believe you," said Yamada, "but how can you do it without telling a lie? If you lie, we'll all be disgraced."

Three hours later, Ferdinand Feghoot returned from the Palace. "Well, it's all fixed," he reported. "No trouble at all. When he asked my opinion, I said, 'Your Highness, where art is concerned, this statuette is simply the Sino-Kwannon.'"

In 3714, when a lovely gray-striped soprano, Tabitha Mewmieeeu, triumphed as Pussy Galore in the folk opera *Son of James Bond*, everyone thought that the cultural integration of the felino-human society of Onderdonck III* was complete. The diva, however, responded to a standing ovation by actually purring the Planetary Anthem and, of course, hell broke loose.

It was the custom to declaim the words of the Anthem very solemnly before they were sung by people and cats. The new arrangement (by noted composer Gilbert Yeowr-hssst, La Mewmieeeu's lover) used no words at all. Human extremists, shaking their fists, insisted that it be universally banned because it could not be spoken. Cat extremists, lashing their tails, proclaimed it the acme of feline art, and demanded full recognition.

Feghoot was called in to arbitrate. He listened to all the

hot arguments, and to Mme. Mew-mieeeu's splendid rendition. Then he gave them his verdict.

"As a work of art, it is simply superb," he declared. "It must be heard down the ages. However, it must always be done unofficially, for its music alone."

"Why?" demanded cats and men with one voice.

"Because," said Ferdinand Feghoot, "we must all admit that, as your Anthem, it is an unspeakable purr-version."

*See Feghoot 47.

When Ferdinand Feghoot was conducting his monumental researches into the curious avian cultures of Parallel Universe C-361,506, he was always disguised as a very large swan, a form which brought him the utmost respect and attention. However, as the natives were addicted to endless philosophical arguments, it was all he could do to keep politely awake; and once he became so thoroughly groggy that, for the very first time, he committed an error in navigating his Space-Time Shuttle.

Instead of arriving safely through the)(at the Time-Travellers Club, he appeared abruptly in a vineyard on the slopes of Olympus—surrounded by a crowd of bucolic Classical Greeks. As his shuttle was disguised as a small thunderstorm, he made quite an impression. His audience was frightened and hostile.

"The bird is a demon!" screeched a gnarled graybeard. "Slay it!"

Immediately, the peasants fitted stones to their slings, brandished billhooks and staves, started advancing. For a moment, his life hung in the balance.

But Feghoot was seldom nonplussed. He reared his long sinuous neck and regarded his attackers with cold, beady eyes. Then he spoke in a vast, terrible voice.

"Take me to your Leda!" said Ferdinand Feghoot.

Oddly enough, it was neither to Duncan Idaho, nor to a Mentat, nor even to his Bene Gesserit mother that Duke Paul Atreides unburdened himself when things lay really heavily on his spirit. On such occasions, he invariably called on Ferdinand Feghoot, to whom he had been introduced by Frank Herbert, a mutual acquaintance.

At the very moment of his triumph over the Imperium, the Desert Mouse of the Fremen invited his friend to a top secret Bene Gesserit picnic and clambake.

"Ferdinand," he said sadly, "I should be rejoicing. Look what we have accomplished. Consider what our world will be like in a very few years. Instead, melancholy overwhelms me. Look about you."

Feghoot did so.

"What you see is important—but far more important to me is what you don't see. Birds, Feghoot—plain, squawking, Audubon Society Earth birds. Someday we'll import them by shiploads, but now we are practically birdless." He sighed dismally.

"You are right, Muad'Dib," murmured Ferdinand Feghoot. "What is so rare as a jay in *Dune?*"

When the Galactic Senate announced, in 2366, that all planets would vote on whether or not to abandon the silver standard, no one was as alarmed as W.J. Bryan Rothschild of New Comstock, a world known as the financial hub of the universe. He at once summoned Ferdinand Feghoot.

"Please save me!" he wept. "My financial empire is based entirely on silver. If we go over to gold, I—who have arranged half the loans in the Galaxy—will be ruined. My signature will never again appear on writ, contract, or even promissory note! Never will I have another occasion to write it. Oh, Ferdinand, it is too terrible to contemplate!"

Feghoot agreed to assist him, and he spent weeks making speeches, writing articles, lobbying, and touring the backplanets. At the last moment, he returned to watch the results in Rothschild's company. They left no doubt as to his effectiveness. Gold was defeated by fourteen to one.

"Saved!" shouted Rothschild, hastily scribbling a check in six figures. "Feghoot, I can hardly believe it—you have triumphed once more!"

"Hi-yo!" replied Feghoot as he took his departure. "This silver ballot means that the Loan Arranger writes again!"

The ideas for this Feghoot and for the three following it won the first four awards in a Feghoot contest sponsored by the Magazine of Fantasy and Science Fiction in 1973.

(with thanks to Thomas C. Gutheil, M.D.)

The planet Gutenberg, a haven for bibliophiles, was soon taken over by unscrupulous rare book dealers, who passed corrupt laws to trap unwary collectors; and in 2203, Ferdinand Feghoot and his friend Andrew Sterling almost fell victim to these. Suddenly they were told that, their visas having expired, they would never be permitted to leave.

"However," leered the official, "I collect inscribed first editions of great English poets. If each of you happened to have—?"

Feghoot drew his despairing companion away. "I have a fake *Prometheus Unbound*, so good that no one can tell it from a real first. Now you hurry off and buy something locally."

"But he—he said inscribed."

"Meet me at the Convent of St. Thomas the Wise* as soon as you can," Feghoot said. "Sister Angelica will take care of it."

At the Convent, he explained to the Sister, who was their greatest calligrapher. He donated generously to their Library Fund, and finally she agreed to furnish the needed inscriptions.

Scarcely had she begun than there was a wild beating on the door. Feghoot opened it. Sterling, excitedly waving a copy of Byron's *Don Juan*, demanded to see Sister Angelica instantly.

Feghoot restrained him. "Wait till the nun signs Shelley," he sang cheerfully.

Thomas James Wise (1859–1937) canonized 2127 on the authority of his biography, Forging Ahead, by Wilfred Partington.

(with thanks to William David Broxon)

At the end of the Missourian Momarchy, when its Women's Lib origins were forgotten and it had fallen under the absolute dictatorship of Supermom, Ferdinand Feghoot faced one of his most dangerous decisions. Supermom (actually Hattie Lou Schultz) had been fertile, producing eighteen healthy babies, most of whom Feghoot had sired. However, none had been girls, and her power was imperiled—for her younger sister, Buzzie Bee, had had female children, and if Supermom failed in what the midwives agreed had to be her last effort, she would depose her immediately.

Finally, with due ceremony, Hattie Lou gave birth to one more hearty infant. Only the midwives (sworn to secrecy) and its father were allowed to behold it until its sex was announced and it had been appropriately garbed. There stood Feghoot, wearing a large medal saying Pop. There was Supermom, with her guards, and her ambitious sister with hers; and he remembered vividly the punishments promised him by his consort—for the child, gurgling in its carefully screened crib, was only too obviously male.

Feghoot thought for only a moment. Then he smiled. "It is my opinion," he announced, "that the good of the state and my personal well-being will be best served if I just skirt the issue."

(with thanks to Paul Major)

Ferdinand Feghoot sadly reported the fate of the Reverend Elmo Milldrip to the Peoria Society for the Conversion of Cannibals.

"I told him the Ngusa were utterly unredeemable, but he just wouldn't listen. God had sent him an infallible ally—John, Lord Greystoke, better known as Tarzan of the Apes, who of course was a real person, very impressive in his lionskin loincloth. 'Mr. Feghoot,' he told me indignantly, when I tried to dissuade them, 'I am still Lord of the Jungle!'

"Swinging from tree to tree, the three of us reached the Ngusi capital where, behind its thorn boma, the natives were preparing a feast; and Greystoke, seizing a vine, uttered the bloodcurdling battle-cry of the Great Apes and launched himself over their heads. Unhappily, he had put on weight in retirement and the vine broke in mid-air. Before our horrified eyes, the cannibals slew him, converted most of him into stew, and dried his intestines, with which they restrung a primitive musical instrument. After the ghastly banquet, their Chief started playing it. He played on and on, and poor Brother Milldrip seemed to be hypnotized. He refused to make his escape, and finally I was forced to abandon him there."

"But why wouldn't he leave?" asked the Chairman.

"He was not only pious," replied Ferdinand Feghoot. "He was also a patriot. He must have believed that the Chief meant to play the Tarzan's tripes forever."

(with thanks to F.M. Busby

By 2133, ten years after an Order in Council invested them with all rights to the entire Sherlock Holmes canon, the Baker Street Irregulars had become a corporation of vast wealth and power. As shareholders, its Members received fat annual dividends, and the privilege of Membership was jealously guarded. When the splendid Conan Doyle Memorial Hall (next to the headquarters at 221-B Baker Street) was officially opened in July of that year, extraordinary precautions were taken to ensure that no outsider should enter. The affair was kept strictly secret; armed guards were posted all 'round the building; every door was heavily padlocked.

Picasso Corstone-Corby, M.D., Grand Master and Chairman of the Board, stepped up to the great main portals, Officers and Members close at his heels. He inserted his huge golden key. He threw open the doors—

There at the podium, very much at his ease, stood Ferdinand Feghoot.

"Who are you, sir?" bellowed Corstone-Corby. "How dare you stand there? Be off with you instantly!"

A tremendous cheer rose from the crowd. "It's Feghoot! It's Ferdinand Feghoot!"

Grudgingly, the doctor gave ground. "Well—harrrumph! Still can't understand it. How the devil did you even hear of this business?"

"Sheer luck," Feghoot said modestly.

"Perhaps so," snapped the doctor. "You still couldn't enter. We had everything padlocked."

Feghoot produced a stout metal-cutter. "Shear lock," he replied.

"But dammit, man, why didn't you simply come to the door and bribe your way in?"

Ruefully, Feghoot spread out his pockets. "Share lack," he explained.

By that time, the Members were shouting and chanting, "We want Feghoot! Make Feghoot a Member!" and even an occasional "Feghoot Grand Master!"

Corstone-Corby recognized that they were in no mood to be trifled with. He called for a vote. It was unanimous.

He bowed. "Mr. Feghoot," said he, "as Grand Master and Chairman of the Board, I take pleasure in welcoming you as an Honorary Life Member and Fellow Shareholder of this Organization. I can see that, like the Great Detective whom we all love and honor, you are a man of vast learning, of incisive intellect, of inflexible logic."

"Just put me down as a Holmespun philosopher," said Ferdinand Feghoot.

FEGHOOT 87

"Editors laugh at my novels!" Little Boguslav Gingko wept into the beer Ferdinand Feghoot had charitably bought him. "I create a great civilization derived not from monkeys but from marsupials—kangaroos, wallabies, koala bears! But no one will publish me! I shall die completely forgotten!"

"Perhaps I can help you," said Feghoot. "There's an alternate universe—" He displayed a gadget like a mini-computer. "—with just such a civilization. Of course, they aren't kangaroo-people—they evolved from native American marsupials. But they have a splendid publishing industry. Shall we go there?"

Eagerly, Gingko agreed. Feghoot made an adjustment. The air glowed blue and whistled—and suddenly they were there. The natives, who except for their tails and pouches looked almost human, welcomed them warmly; and less than

a week later their most important editor personally accepted all Gingko's novels. "They're magnificent!" he declared.
"Never have I read such stark realism!"

As they left, Gingko sighed. "Do you think I will really
make literary history?" he asked. "Will I be remembered and
read long after I'm dead?"

"My dear fellow," said Ferdinand Feghoot, "I assure you
that all your works will be published possumously."

After the Children of Israel had wandered for thirty-nine years in the wilderness, Ferdinand Feghoot arrived to make sure that they would finally find and enter the Promised Land. With him he brought his favorite robot, faithful old Yewtoo Artoo, to carry his gear and do assorted camp chores.

The Israelites soon got over their initial fear of the robot and, as the months passed, became very fond of him. Patriarchs took to discussing abstruse theological problems with him, and each evening the children all gathered to hear the many stories with which he was programmed. Therefore it came as a great shock to them when, just as their journey was ending, he abruptly wore out. Even Feghoot couldn't console them.

"It may be true, Ferdinand Feghoot," said Moses, "that our friend Yewtoo Artoo was soulless, but we cannot believe it. He must be properly interred. We cannot embalm him as do the Egyptians. Nor have we wood for a coffin. But I do have a most splendid skin from one of Pharaoh's own cattle. We shall bury him in it."

Feghoot agreed. "Yes, let this be his last rusting place."

"Rust?" Moses cried. "Not in this dreadful dry desert!"

"Ah," sighed Ferdinand Feghoot, shedding a tear. "I fear you do not realize the full significance of Pharaoh's ox hide."

In 2147, after conquering the one hundred countries surrounding his capital, the mighty Bwasimba I proclaimed himself Emperor of Africa and announced a grand feast of celebration by the banks of his ancestral Ngusi River.

"One problem remains," he told Ferdinand Feghoot. "An anthem worthy of me and my fame. But don't worry—our delectable freshwater eels are an unfailing source of omens and oracles."

Tables were set for the Court, and tens of thousands of subjects thronged the high riverside cliffs. Suddenly, excited shouts interrupted their cheering. The Imperial Fishermen had come with their catch, dancing triumphantly—and their ancient chief carried the biggest, most splendid eel ever seen!

Instantly, the crowd went out of control. They swept the old man off his feet. He lost his grip on the huge, squirming eel—which fell off the cliff and was lost again in the river. Bwasimba, ecstatic a moment before, bellowed in anguish.

"Calm yourself, Serene Highness," soothed Feghoot. "All is not lost. You now have your anthem—the 'Marseillaise!'"

"For that wretched mob?" roared Bwasimba. "It's too good for them! They lost me the finest eel in the world!"

"Exactly," said Ferdinand Feghoot. "That was your oracle. Wasn't it a mob that brought about the fall of the best eel?"

One of history's best kept military secrets was how Ferdinand Feghoot helped Sir Robert Baden-Powell (who founded the Boy Scouts) to hold out during the seven-month siege of Mafeking in the Boer War.

"We must ally ourselves with South Africa's army ants," he told the commander. "They're highly intelligent, and their martial spirit is equal to ours. They'll be delighted."

Sir Robert was dubious, so Feghoot took him outside, where a large detachment of army ants was engaged in maneuvers.

"They're very rank conscious," he explained. "If we don't address the proper commander, they'll ignore us completely. Now watch the first platoon there—"

The head of the column advanced. Then abruptly the first ant turned left. When the second one followed him, Feghoot spoke up. "I say," he remarked, "why don't you lads go off and make life miserable for the Boers out there?"

At once, the ant halted. He waved his mandibles peremptorily. And the whole column marched off in the other direction.

"Astounding!" Sir Robert exclaimed. "Captain, how on earth did you know that was the platoon leader?"

"It was simple, sir," said Ferdinand Feghoot. "I addressed myself to the second left turn ant."

Ferdinand Feghoot and Augustus the Strong, King of Poland, were boon companions for a number of years, indulging in many a high revel together. (Indeed, Feghoot was godfather to more than a score of the King's three hundred and fifty-two illegitimate children.)

Only once was their friendship endangered. Augustus, who always consulted Feghoot on serious military matters, had reorganized his personal bodyguard, arming them with the finest halberds obtainable. The huge blades, twice as broad as a headsman's axe, had been forged in Toledo; their immensely long staffs had been cleverly fashioned from black oak by the craftsmen of Nuremberg. Because he had not bothered to tell Feghoot about this, envious courtiers saw their opportunity and started a whispering campaign, telling the King that his friend was ridiculing the halberds and making all sorts of coarse jests about them.

"Ferdinand," growled Augustus, obviously hurt and offended, "those beautiful weapons are my pride and joy—how could you make fun of them?"

"Your Majesty!" cried Ferdinand Feghoot in outrage. "Surely you cannot believe such a lie! Do you think that I, of all people, would tell poleaxe jokes at your court?"

Had it not been for Ferdinand Feghoot's quick thinking, Sir Richard Burton would never have become famous as the first Unbeliever to reach Mecca, and his translation of the Arabian Nights never would have been published. Feghoot (who had made the trip many times over the centuries) kindly went with him, posing as a humble used-camel dealer.

As the caravan started out, the fierce desert sheik who was convoying it stared at Burton suspiciously. "Who is this man, Honest Akbar?" he demanded. "He doesn't look like a Moslem to me."

"He's a Pathan from faraway Hind," Feghoot told him. "That is why his appearance and accent are strange."

The sheik glared for a moment and galloped away, and poor Burton sighed in relief. Then, at the midday halt, when they were all called to prayer, he made his mistake. He threw down his prayer rug and prostrated himself—not to the East, like everyone else, but to the West!

Instantly the sheik and his men were upon him, their scimitars drawn, shrieking, "Slay him! Slay the uncircumcised infidel!"

"Stop!" shouted Ferdinand Feghoot in the nick of time. "O Sons of the Prophet, he didn't do it on purpose! He's just Occident prone!"

FEGHOOT 93

"I'm so glad you've returned, Mr. Feghoot," said Queen Victoria, as they sipped Highland whiskey in her sitting room at Balmoral Castle. "We do have a most difficult problem."

"Och, aye," declared John Brown, her devoted Scottish gamekeeper and friend. "It's that domned poacher, ye ken."

"You mean you still haven't caught him?" asked Feghoot.

"Sir, the problem is we have caught him—that is, we ken weel who he is, and there's naught to be done about it. He's Sir Andrew MacHaggis, Lord Chief Justice of Scotland, and there's scarce a day when he doesn't shoot a good dozen of our cock pheasants. Then he hides the birrds in a hole in the wall, and comes here bold as brass to pay his reespects. He desairves to be shot, but ye canna shoot a Lord Chief Justice of Scotland."

"No," sighed the Queen. "Nor can we drag him to court

like a common criminal. We must think of public opinion. Yet punished he must be. Oh, Mr. Feghoot, what shall we do?"

Feghoot thought for a moment. Then, "Your Majesty," he announced, "I have a solution of which I'm sure Prince Albert would have approved. You can charge Sir Andrew quite properly with male pheasants in orifice."

FEGHOOT 94

Cleopatra II, the Mad Queen of Egypt, had periods of relative sanity during her long reign, and during one of these she wisely appointed Ferdinand Feghoot her Defense Minister and Astrologer-General.

"Feghoot Pasha," she said, "never has Egypt been in such peril. The forces of that cruel dictator, who calls himself the New Idi Amin and boasts of his utter ruthlessness, are even now massing to invade us. We have just received the latest of his insulting messages. Listen!"

The Minister of Foreign Affairs read it aloud: "I, the New Idi Amin, am coming. I am coming with fire and sword, to lay waste your land, to slay man, woman, and child. Surrender at once! This is your last opportunity! Never, foolish Queen, can your miserable troops withstand my vast armored forces!"

"Shall I surrender?" whimpered the Queen. "What hope has my little army against him?"

"Have no fear, Your Majesty," declared Ferdinand Feghoot. "It is not only in the stars that we read the future. It also is mirrored in the past. This man is what the Chinese used to call a paper tiger. You need never quail before his armored forces. The key lies in Egypt's long history. Haven't you heard of Two-Tank-Amin?"

During the science fiction boom of the late 1980s, Ferdinand Feghoot became Executive Managing Editor-in-Chief of an entire chain of famous magazines: Tri-Sexual Space Tales, Future Porn, Abysmal Monster Stories, and any number of others. Most of his writers, of course, sent their work in by interfax, but Frieda Claptrap, the militant feminist, absolutely refused. Three or four times a week, she came stamping into his office in her lumberjack boots, and sometimes she picketed the building for days at a time, carrying placards accusing his male editors of being chauvinist pigs and their female counterparts of being their sex-slaves; and always she came loaded with more and more manuscripts.

Before many months had gone by, staff efficiency began to drop sharply. Resignations, hard drinking, and nervous breakdowns took their toll. It became harder and harder to make deadlines. Then one day Feghoot came back from lunch to find the building seething with excitement and police. In the middle was a disheveled Ms. Claptrap, screaming she'd been raped by all the men on the staff while all the women did nothing to help her.

"Is this true, Mr. Feghoot?" asked the inspector in charge. "Was this really a gang rape?"

"I hardly think so," replied Ferdinand Feghoot. "I suspect it was simply a multiple submission."

Ferdinand Feghoot,
  poet in German meadow,
he calls out, "Hi, *kuh!*"

Shortly after Ferdinand Feghoot undertook the psychotherapy of Cleopatra II of Egypt in 2054, he encountered one of those desperate emergencies with which only he could successfully cope. The Queen, having restructured Egyptian society after the pattern of Aldous Huxley's Brave New World, had forced all her subjects to worship Henry Ford and, reverently, to make the Sign of the T. Her most sacred relic, a genuine 1913 Model T touring car, had been carefully restored and she decided to enshrine it, with due ceremony, in the Great Pyramid: she herself, her courtiers and guards, and the whole population of Cairo accompanied the Holy Vehicle, which was driven by the Royal Chauffeur, old Mustafa.

She had issued orders that, under pain of death, no words other than Huxley's were to be uttered, so the procession was impressively silent. Then, abruptly, halfway, a dreadful desert wind struck them, blasting sand in their eyes and blowing off hats and tarbooshes. It tore away one of the straps holding the Model T's top, and everyone held his breath, for the aged chauffeur had not even noticed. They knew how terrible the Queen's rage would be if it blew off completely, but none dared cry out a warning.

They needn't have worried.

"Tie Mustafa's top!" shouted Ferdinand Feghoot.

Many years after Ferdinand Feghoot discovered the *dzop*, the strange flying bird-plants of Golightly III, he was asked by Dr. Gropius Volkswagen, a fellow member of the Time Travelers Club, how he had saved himself when the queen of the abominable aborigines demanded that he catch freshly laid *dzop* eggs and make ritual charms out of them.

"It was really quite easy," Feghoot told him. "*Dzop* eggs are modified seed pods, under enormous pressure. When the flocks find their blue nesting trees, this becomes unendurable. Then each *dzop* aims her tail at her tree and lets go. The eggs bury themselves in the trees at a velocity of over 2800 feet per second. Trying to catch them would be exceedingly hazardous, but I could never have admitted this because the Queen thought me a mighty magician, so I just pointed out that you can't make an amulet without breaking eggs."*

"But how were you sure you couldn't have caught them?" the doctor persisted. "Did you actually try?"

"Of course not," said Ferdinand Feghoot. "I was simply giving the Queen my egg-spurt opinion."

*See Feghoot 24.

In 2037, the Give the Country Back to the Indians Party elected the President and Vice-President, captured both houses of Congress, and even persuaded the Indians to accept.

Sweeping changes were instituted. Palefaces (all who were less than one-sixteenth Indian) were moved to remote reservations, where they were allowed to perform quaint tribal dances and sell souvenirs to tourists. However, they were strictly forbidden Indian cultural materials—eagle feathers, especially.

The first Paleface charged with this crime was one Angus MacGillicuddy, who had used three eagle feathers in what he called "a Highland war bonnet," and Ferdinand Feghoot defended him before the Supreme Council of Sachems and Medicine Chiefs.

To their astonishment, he summoned the prosecutor himself, Melvin B. Many Thunders, as his sole witness. "Sir," he said, "my client denies that he feloniously obtained these feathers. He avers that he picked them up from the ground in all innocence. Now, isn't it true that a sick eagle generally molts, losing feathers?"

"What of it?" scoffed Many Thunders. "Try proving this guy ever came anywhere near a sick eagle."

"Prove it?" purred Ferdinand Feghoot. "You yourself have admitted it! It's all in the record. When you denounced Mr. MacGillicuddy, you declared they were ill eagle feathers!"

In the fifth year of the reign of Hamid al-Hazred XXVII (Hamid the Insufferable), the planet Mars was kidnapped bodily out of the Solar System. All the mullahs and every dissident element at once started screaming, and the distraught Sultan turned to Feghoot for help.

"Imagine it, Feghoot Bey!" he bellowed, rending his beard. "I spend trillions of piastres terraforming that planet, installing planet heaters, even a substitute sun—and these miserable mullahs accuse me of stealing it—of turning it into my private seraglio! I've tried impaling them and drowning them in the Bosphorus—and it does no good at all. If you can prove to them that someone else did it, you can have any reward you desire!"

"Five hundred Circassian virgins?" Feghoot asked modestly.

"I'll write out the requisition at once!"

Feghoot smiled. "Merciful Majesty, the real culprits are your ancient enemies, the Russians. A secret Russian underground group known as The Brotherhood has been plotting the dark deed for ages. They've even boasted about it!" "Give me proof!" roared the Sultan.

"That's simple," said Ferdinand Feghoot. "Centuries ago one of their writers, Dostoevski, actually published a book called *The Brothers Carry Mars Off*."

In 1908, shortly before the death of the formidable Empress Dowager, Tzu Hsi, Ferdinand Feghoot sentimentally tried to save her doomed Chinese Empire. (He had ruled as the Emperor Fei Hu, 357–329 B.C.) Though she paid no heed to his counsels, his mission was by no means an absolute failure. He did save the life of her Master Chef, venerable Mao Shih-Pen.

A young lion had escaped from the zoo, and the Empress decreed that when it was cornered and shot it would be the piece de résistance at a most splendid banquet. The top mandarins were invited, and the whole diplomatic corps. After any number of delicate dishes were served, finally in came Mao's masterpiece.

Everyone set to eagerly—and there was a sudden dead silence. The dish tasted awful. The French ambassador actually spat his first bite into his napkin.

The furious Empress had Mao dragged before her. "Such insulting incompetence," she screamed, "must be punished!" And she sentenced him to suffer the death of a thousand cuts.

Instantly, Feghoot threw himself at her feet. "Be merciful, Heavenbom!" he cried out. "Master Mao wasn't responsible. Your political enemies have been spiking his tea with straight alcohol! He was drunk without knowing it!"

"How do you know this?" she demanded.

"It was obvious," replied Ferdinand Feghoot. "The poor old man couldn't even wok a strayed lion."

One of Ferdinand Feghoot's favorite haunts, a Time-Travellers Club rendezvous where they told magnificent tales, was a saloon called The Bilge Pump. In the 1980s, however, it became infested by an odd group of science fictionadoes, writers trying to pilfer story ideas and addicts scrounging fringe benefits, all arguing bitterly about who did what first.

Old Juniper Widget, author of Regurgitations from the Glob Galaxy, boasted that he had once pinched H.G. Wells; even older Veronica Lewdski bragged of being the first woman seduced in a submarine—by a grandnephew of Jules Verne at that; young Pat Squirrell claimed his granddad had organized the first SF convention just before McKinley's election.

One evening, Feghoot appeared among them garbed as a Japanese Buddhist priest. "Bah!" he exclaimed. "Newcomers! I have just returned from the century of Japan's civil wars. When I started my wanderings, my friend Norimitsu the swordsmith was worried. 'Feghoot-sama,' he said, 'though a priest wears no sword, no man should go unarmed in these evil times. Allow me to forge you an uchtwa—a steel warfan. With it, because of the virtue and strength of my name, you can smite any assailant.' Of course, I accepted." Feghoot produced the heavy steel weapon. "Here it is. See how he signed it? Bishu Ju Norimitsu, Choroku 3rd Year."

"What's that got to do with SF?" shrilled Ms. Lewdski.

"Choroku 3rd Year," said Ferdinand Feghoot, "was 1460 A.D. That is the date of the first Feghoot fan club."

In 3227, the Society for the Aesthetic Rearrangement of History presented its coveted Tempus Award to Ferdinand Feghoot. "Mr. Feghoot," said Dr. Corydon Bramahpootra, its President, "by going back to 1819 and saving Reverend Sylvester Gerbil of the London Missionary Society from the enraged natives of Navinavi, you prevented the South Seas disaster that followed his death in all other continua. Besides, armed only with a fowling piece and a boar spear, you held the primitives off until the return of your time-shuttle. You are truly a hero!"

Feghoot accepted the award—an antique alarm clock in amber—to tumultuous applause. "I wasn't really heroic," he said modestly. "I just didn't like the alternative."

"Dear Mr. Feghoot!" shrilled a small, twittering newsperson. "Those dreadful savages were supposed to be cannibals would they really have eaten you?"

"Well," he replied, "their cannibalism wasn't only for protein. It was ritualistic. If they admired you as an adversary, they would gobble up just certain parts—to acquire your strength, wisdom, and courage."

"The beasts! Didn't you just simply loathe them?"

"Why should I?" said Ferdinand Feghoot. "They were men after my own heart."

For years, Ferdinand Feghoot maintained an affectionate relationship with Mrs. Pigafetta, a middle-aged Sicilian mermaid who kept a penzione for shipwrecked sailors on an island near Taranto. On summer evenings, they sat together at the door of her commodious waterside cavern, singing sentimental operatic arias.

Then once, on arriving, he found her in tears. "Cherubino mio," she sobbed, "today I cannot sing, even for you. Inflation destroys me—yes, even here on my island! How shall I pay for my pasta, bologna, red wine, to feed the poor sailors the sea brings to me?"

Feghoot thought for a moment. "You have another cavern under this, don't you? Below sea level? You've told me that fish are very intelligent. Why not rent it to them? They could pay you with pearls, or with small fish for your table."

"Never!" she cried. "The great greedy flat fish would move in at once—manta rays, sting-rays, the rest! They would eat up my profits. I would have to put up a sign to prevent them. Then my sailors would say, 'You board fish in the basement—this is a disorderly house!' They would all swim away."

"Not if you put up a sign they're used to, cara mia, one that doesn't seem to apply to any kind of fish."

"Can there be such?" She flicked tears away with her tail.

"No Skate-Boarding," said Ferdinand Feghoot.

FEGHOOT 105

In 1597, the Sultan Mahommed III, impressed by British victories over the power of Spain, sent Queen Elizabeth a magnificent boa constrictor as a token of his esteem. Never had such a huge and beautifully marked serpent been seen in England, and at first the Queen was much taken by it. Francis Bacon and Ferdinand Feghoot designed a vast iron snakehouse for it, and she proudly displayed it to her favorites and to foreign ambassadors.

Almost from the beginning, however, she was tormented by ominous dreams, all of which seemed to originate with the snake. Finally, she summoned the bold Earl of Essex. "Have the headsman destroy it!" she ordered.

"Headsman?" cried the Earl. "Your Majesty, I fear no mere serpent. To serve you, I shall slay it myself!"

Feghoot went with him. Servants were summoned, carrying spades for its burial, and the intrepid Earl entered the cage, where the boa was sleepily digesting a fat Southdown ewe. With one blow of his broadsword, he struck off its head.

"Ferdinand Feghoot," he exulted, as it writhed in its death agonies. "Now our Virgin Queen once more will dream only sweet dreams! She'll see me as a second St. George, and my place in her heart will always be secure!"

"Be not so sure, my lord," said Ferdinand Feghoot, who of course knew of the sad fate awaiting the Earl. "Who knows what dreams may come when we have shoveled off this mottled coil?"

The greatest years in the reign of Haroun al-Rashid were those when Ferdinand Feghoot was his Grand Vizier, and the Caliph blundered only when he refused to take Feghoot's advice.

Once Sindbad the Sailor returned from far Æthopia with news of a wonderful beast.

"It is like a fine horse of Araby," proclaimed the Caliph, "silver-coated, golden-maned. But that isn't all—from its brow grows a horn of true ivory! I am sending Scheherazade's favorite slave, cunning old Farouk, to capture one for me."

"I know of these creatures, Your Magnificence," Feghoot replied. "But Farouk? Surely not. Only a virgin can tame one."

"Tame one?" laughed the Caliph. "I have no wish to tame them. They shall be bred in captivity. All Farouk has to do is to catch it."

After three long years, Farouk and Sindbad returned, and with them, ramping and snorting in its cage, was their quarry.

"I told you so, Feghoot!" Haroun crowed. "Look at—" He broke off. "What have you done, wretched Farouk?" he roared. "This miserable beast has been gelded!" Raging, he drew his jeweled scimitar from its scabbard.

Feghoot intervened bravely. "Stay your hand, Protector of the Poor!" he cried out. "What do you expect? Old Farouk was a harem employee. Of course he brought you a eunuchorn!"

"Ferdinand Feghoot," said Henry VIII, when Feghoot answered his summons early in 1543, "All this sweet spring I have courted Catherine Parr, Lord Latimer's widow. I adore her and would make her my Queen, but she'll have none of me. She says I'm a grim fellow with whom she fears she can never be merry or lie at ease—and all because I had to have two of my wives put to death. I cannot persuade her that this was not the real me, bluff King Hal, but their own infidelity. Go you to her. Because all know you always speak truth, she will believe you when you tell her what a fine cheery monarch I am, and what a jolly husband I'll make her."

Feghoot bowed, took horse, and set off on his mission, and on his return it was Henry himself who greeted him at the gates of the palace.

"Feghoot!" he cried out. "Did'st thou score?"

"Aye, won over Parr!" came the answer.

"God bless you!" The delighted Henry at once stripped a jeweled gold chain from his shoulders and placed it around Feghoot's. "What did you tell her?"

"The simple truth, Your Majesty," said Ferdinand Feghoot. "I said you were a veritable Bluebeard of happiness."

Ferdinand Feghoot incurred the enmity of Dr. Gropius Volkswagen, then President of the Society for the Aesthetic Rearrangement of History, when that elderly scholar presented his monumental paper on "Saving the World by Removing the Internal Combustion Engine from the Twentieth Century."

He listened politely until comments were called for. Then he addressed himself to the podium. "My dear Doctor," he said, "while I appreciate the depth of your learning and your mountains of data, I must take issue with a few of your points."

Dr. Volkswagen sneered.

"The Datsun was not, as you've stated, 'a long German dog with short legs used to hunt badgers.' Nor did the Audubon Society conduct high-speed races on Germany's freeways. Finally, the novel Vespers in Vienna was not concerned with the Austrian importation of Italian motor-scooters."

Dr. Volkswagen's face grew redder and redder. "SO!" he exploded. "By quibbling you think you make a monkey out of Gropius Volkswagen, Ph.D., Ph.D., Ph.D.? I am right. If we do not the filthy internal combustion engine remove, it is the end of the world!"

"That would be a shame!" said Ferdinand Feghoot. "To end not with a bang, not with a whimper, but just with a Saab."

FEGHOOT 109

"**F**erdinand Feghoot, to our advanced science Earth's problem is simple," declared the head of the Medical Mission from the planet Yuck III, waving his stethoscope-tentacles. "It is constipation! We had only to view your advertisements—Ex-Lax, Nose-Lax, Milk of Magnesia—I know not what! Now we shall go back to our nice healthy planet where no one is constipated."

Feghoot, who had been appointed by the Reconstituted United Nations to give the Mission every facility, did not comment.

"However," continued the Yuckian, "because you have treated us very respectfully, we shall give you a present. Earthmen will no longer suffer from this terrible ailment." He gestured to one of his staff, who immediately opened a carrying case and extracted two gopher-like animals with shoe-button eyes and wiggly brown noses.

"Behold! These are two *clenj*. They multiply very rapidly—before long every Earthman can have one. A single whiff of their breath, which smells terrible—poof! no more constipation. Also they are very affectionate. They will be your true friends. I trust you are all properly grateful."

"I assure you that we will be, dear Doctor," said Ferdinand Feghoot. "With friends like that, who needs enemas?"

When Ferdinand Feghoot went back to 1908 to delay the fall of the Chinese Empire (he ruled as the Emperor Fei Hu, 357–329 s.c.), his efforts were frustrated by the Empress Dowager, old Tzu Hsi, who refused all advice. He, however, loyally acceded to every one of her wishes.

Finally, she revealed her plans to him. "The Foreign Devils plotting my downfall," she screamed, "shall never succeed! I have formed a corps of one thousand brave women warriors, tall, strong, handsome girls from the North, armed with our traditional jingals. They shall terrify the Barbarians!"

Jingals were huge, obsolete muzzle-loaders firing inch-and-a-half balls, but Feghoot was too wise to argue.

"My women must have stirring music to parade to," she went on. "Choose it! Teach my military musicians to play it!"

Feghoot promptly set to work, and three weeks later the parade took place outside the Forbidden City. Every foreign ambassador was invited.

Feghoot himself, pleading ear trouble, did not attend, but immediately afterwards he was summoned before the ecstatic ruler. "Did we prevail, oh Daughter of Heaven?" he asked.

"The mere sight of my women and the terror inspired by your music threw the Foreign Devils into utter dismay!" she replied. "Some gaped or cried out. Others clapped their hands to their ears. What do you call that wonderful music?"

"It is called Jingal Belles," said Ferdinand Feghoot.

When the redoubtable Esmeralda Birdbath, Executive Professor of English Literature and Gracious Living at Weekatonk University, assumed the Presidency of the Society of the Aesthetic Rearrangement of History, she at once sent Ferdinand Feghoot off to 2882 to learn whether her pet program—for the Butlerization of Literary Criticism—was to succeed.

"I must know!" she cried. "Return instantly, to this precise moment!" And she herself pushed him into the Society's)(.

A tense few minutes later, he reappeared.

"You have triumphed!" he announced. "In 2882, Samuel Butler's great dictum of the true test of literary genius is not the ability to write an inscription but the ability to name a kitten dominates all literary criticism, and I'm happy to say that I, in the three weeks I spent there, won their much-coveted Samuel Butler Memorial Gold Medal by doing so. I and five hundred others were in the finals, and the names we chose had to reflect our kittens' backgrounds and breeds. They brought me a delightful blue-point Siamese, a tom, and I named him instantly—Levi Strauss—to tremendous applause."

"But that's absurd!" she snapped. "A Jewish name could have nothing to do with that kitten's heredity!"

"On the contrary, dear Esmeralda," said Ferdinand Feghoot. "I called him that because of his blue genes."

FEGHOOT 112

"It is an oudraitch!" screamed Dr. Gropius Volkswagen. "I myself, Chairman of the Society for the Aesthetic Rearrangement of History, sent this Ferdinand Feghoot back to 1985, to this kibbutz on the West Bank, where history is so untidy. He was away much too long, and we received only one brief message from him. We all thought he was risking his miserable life every day to tidy things up. Now a confidential informant has told us that during his whole stay there was only peace and tranquility. No rockets! No Arab terrorists! And do you know what he was doing, this brave Feghoot? Ha! He was operating agricultural machinery! Also he was running the kibbutz's rabbit farm!"

The Society, of course, voted unanimously to summon Feghoot to defend himself, and he duly appeared before them.

"Here is the man who has wasted our money!" Dr. Volkswagen bellowed. "Here is the hero who let us believe he was risking his life every minute! Feghoot, what can you say for yourself?"

"My dear Doctor," said Ferdinand Feghoot. "My message made no such claims. Surely you recorded what I said on the trans-temporal telephone? Goodness knows I said it clearly enough. I told you that much of the time I spent there was harrowing, and that I was having many hare-raising experiences. I also asserted quite truthfully that evenings and holidays were always a time of hora."

Ferdinand Feghoot was an intimate friend of Ben Jonson's and spent many a merry evening in the great playwright's company, usually at the Court of James II. It was on one such occasion that the King had—albeit grudgingly—to award him a baronetcy.

The King had been marveling at the profundity of John Donne, then Dean of St. Paul's, to whose homilies he frequently listened. "No philosopher can hold a candle to him!" he averred. "Nay, not even the great Grecians—not even Aristotle! Even he couldn't express such vast truths in such very few words. Why, just last Sunday, Donne uttered one I shall never forget. He said, 'No man is an island.' Who can fault so noble a statement?"

"Your Majesty," replied Feghoot, "it's all right as far as it goes, but it's not wholly accurate."

"Ridiculous!" cried the King. "Fferdinande Ffeghoote, I'll make you a wager. Prove what you say, and you'll be a baronet. Fail, and you'll serve as my headsman for the space of three months."

"Ha!" laughed Ben Jonson. "That'll teach you the meaning of accuracy!"

"I accept your terms, Sire." Feghoot sank to one knee in front of the King. "'No man is an island?' Dr. Donne forgot the one those fine tailless cats come from."

It was Ferdinand Feghoot who introduced Mozart to Mary Jo Scroggs, who inspired one of his most famous operas.

"Your genius isn't declining," he told the despondent composer. "Operas have become too effete, too pretentious. You need to capture the verve of the lower classes—but of course without any embarrassing complications. I know just the girl, and she lives only two centuries away."

As Mary Jo stepped from the time-shuttle in her pretty little flour-sack frock, Mozart was instantly smitten. He boasted to everyone in Vienna of her pert little nose, her impertinent breasts, tiny waist, and pattable bottom. Finally, when it came time for her to return to the Tennessee Mountains, "My dear," he cried, "Ferdinand has sworn that you'll see my new work. I could never have done it without you!"

And the first question he asked when his friend came back a month later was, "Tell me, what did she think of it?"

"She liked the music," Feghoot reported. "She said it was 'durn near as good as a country rock hoe-down.' But when I looked at her after final curtain, she was crying."

"Crying?" Mozart was stricken. "But why?"

"Well," said Ferdinand Feghoot, "you went on so about what a cute shape she had, she 'jest reckoned you oughta of called it *The Figure of Mary Jo.*'"

It would be impossible to overestimate Ferdinand Feghoot's influence on the late 20th Century's serious literature. As an example, when Philip Roth wrote his monumental autobiography in the 1990s, it was to Feghoot that his publisher went for advice on its title.

"Ferdinand," he said almost hysterically, "poor Philip has poured his soul into this book. It tells his trials and adversities, his disappointments and inadequacies, his most painful embarrassments, his despairs, all his mental and physical sufferings. It is tremendously moving and immensely profound, yet we know that without a suitable title it may not succeed. When he wrote *Portnoy's Complaint*, he had no trouble at all. I think it's because the title itself aroused the sympathy of the book buyers."

"That may be part of it," Feghoot replied, "but don't forget—a title must also have that ineffable something that tells you instantly it's going to be a bestseller."

"I know," groaned the unhappy publisher, "but what? We've been getting nowhere. Please, say you can help us!"

"My dear fellow, it's simple," said Ferdinand Feghoot. "Just call it *The Gripes of Roth*."

"I'm terribly worried, Ferdinand Feghoot," sighed Ronald Reagan during the last week of his presidency. "The minute I'm out of the White House, Congress is going hog-wild. Spend, spend, spend! Where will the money come from?"

"Never fear," said Feghoot. "By 1991, genetic engineering will have solved the whole problem."

"Do you mean by changing the people?"

"Not at all. By growing completely new trees—leafless, burgeoning with Federal Reserve notes in every denomination."

"Corne, come!" Reagan protested. "Money doesn't grow on trees!"

Feghoot smiled. "Just let me get to my time shuttle."

In eight hours, he returned, bearing what looked like a small maple tree, except that instead of leaves it was covered with hundred-dollar bills.

"There you are!" he announced. "Each with its own serial number. There'll be an unending harvest to divvy up with every branch of the government."

"It's a miracle!" Reagan cried. "What will they call it?"

"It will be known," said Ferdinand Feghoot, "as the great dividend, Ron."

Ferdinand Feghoot was the first editor of *Weird Tales* (from eight in the morning, when the office opened, until nine twenty-seven, when the publisher made his appearance).

"Feghoot!" the publisher bellowed as he threw open the door. "What have you done? Where is my bookkeeper, Sandy MacDougall? Where is my old secretary, Miss Tiptinkle?"

Feghoot smiled. "I sacked them. MacDougall was a canny Scot. Had he been an uncanny Scot he would've fitted in nicely."

"And who is that—that creature squirming in your lap?"

He pointed at a scantily clad young woman whose lovely sinuous arms were entwined around Feghoot's neck.

"She's my old friend, Millie Henbane. She loves me. See how she kisses me under each ear? How she caresses my neck and nuzzles under my chin?"

"Dammit, a business office is no place for romance!"

"Sir, you don't understand. Dear Millie belongs here. She a neckromancer."

"My God!" the publisher shouted. "Are you trying to bankrupt me before I even get started?"

"Indeed not," said Ferdinand Feghoot, pointing at a tall, turbanned figure muttering ghastly spells over an old vellum tome. "Abdul has it arranged. You're covered against every contingency. We call it Al-Hazred insurance."

When he was writing his famous Royal Fireworks Music in 1747, Handel was terribly resentful of Ferdinand Feghoot, Master of His Majesty's Pyrotechnics, for the King had insisted he consult Feghoot every inch of the way.

"Your Machesty!" he cried out. "Feghoot knows noding of music! How can he tell me vot to write?"

A chamberlain pointed out that Feghoot was simply describing the fireworks so the music might enhance and ennoble them, but Handel shook his head angrily. "Nein! Such a fraud! They are too big! They are imbossible! He bromises pie in der sky!"

Feghoot just smiled.

The great night came. It seemed as if half of London had gathered at Greenpark. Then, sometimes singly, sometimes in veritable regiments, the fireworks released bursts of light, dazzling sprays of color. Wonder followed wonder.

Finally, Feghoot looked at the King and at Handel. "So I promised pie in the sky, did I?" he said. "Very well!"

Simultaneously, rockets soared. Simultaneously, they burst into letters thirty feet high. 3.1416+! they read.

"See?" said Ferdinand Feghoot.

After the great Tokyo stock market crash of 2019, Shigeo Yamaguchi, Japan's richest industrialist, found himself totally bankrupt. He summoned Ferdinand Feghoot, his confidential secretary. "Feghoot," he declared, "I must now commit ritual suicide in accordance with the ancient tradition of stock markets. At high noon, I shall hurl myself from the top floor of my 367-story Yamaguchi Tower, which I no longer own. But the vulgar press must not witness this. You must bring Junji Ono, our greatest photographer. He alone is fit to immortalize my last moments. Tell him nothing. I want him to feel the full impact of the tragedy."

"Hai!" said Feghoot obediently, and presently returned with the mystified Ono, who took one horrified look at Yamaguchi, now clinging to the windowsill by his fingertips, and cried out, "Sir, why is O-Yamaguchi-san dangling there so far in the air?"

Feghoot explained the situation, and after a few hasty words Ono hurried away.

"What's happened?" demanded the suicide. "Why isn't he taking the photograph?"

"Because he is a true artist!" said Ferdinand Feghoot. "He asks that you please be patient and wait. Please graciously try to hang on. He had to go home for his *why dangle lens*."

In the early 1990s, when the Soviet Empire was going through its trauma of democratization instituted by Mikhael Gorbachev, economic conditions became really desperate and Gorbachev was forced to call on Ferdinand Feghoot (in whom Raisa placed full confidence) for assistance.

Feghoot flew at once to St. Petersburg. (He had been in the 16th Century trying to advise Ivan the Terrible.) But he had, of course, already evaluated the situation.

"Oh, what shall I do?" Gorbachev cried, as they drove off in his limousine. "The rouble is worthless. Foreigners sneer at it. Our own people won't touch it. Please, Ferdinand Grendelovitch, you must help me!"

"It's simple, Mikhael Sergeivitch," replied Feghoot. "Your rouble is not dead. It merely reflects the dreadful dull apathy of your masses, crushed by seventy years of Communist tyranny. Waken them! Once they are aroused, believe—the rouble will rouse with them! You must become more democratic, like Yeltsin! I promise you—you will go down in history as a great rouble rouser!"

When the first expedition to Algol released the astounding report of its discovery—that Algol, instead of being a single star, had been split into three, and that these, instead of separating, continued in close proximity to each other in what an enthusiastic French journalist referred to as un jolt menage a trois—the press and the scientific world immediately demanded to know how Ferdinand Feghoot had been able to predict it years before when the expedition set out.

Their demand was fueled by embarrassment, for they had been ridiculing him ever since as a latter-day Velikovsky; and now some of them actually dared to hint that, violating every rule of the Time Travelers Club, he had simply sneaked ahead to find out.

"Utter rot!" exclaimed Feghoot indignantly. "I had just returned from old Rome, where I go periodically to advise Julius Caesar on strategy, and it was he who told me. As he of course spoke no English, he said it in Latin, but it was instantly clear when I translated it. 'Algol is divided into three parts.' He'd undoubtedly heard it from some Grecian philosopher who'd been dipping into the lost scientific knowledge of Atlantis."

Ferdinand Feghoot, at one stroke, solved the terrible economic problems confronting the Russians after the break-up of the Soviet Empire.

"It was simple," he said. "I hurried to Moscow as soon as Boris Yeltsin appealed to me, and found him almost hysterical. 'Ferdinand Grendelovitch!' he cried. 'My economists, the press, even the simplest mujiks in the street—all scream at me, Privatize! Privatize! Already we have McDonald's, stock brokers, S&Ls, mail order houses, just like Poughkeepsie, New York. And still nothing works!'

"I at once understood. The Russian Mafia had taken over, draining the economy. 'My dear Boris," I said, 'you have no KGB. They have all joined the Mafia. But you have replaced them with nothing. They are stealing you blind. But don't worry. I know what you need—what your people are screaming for. They knew it instinctively. Here—'"

I gave him my business card:

Feghoot Security Agency

Trained Confidential Investigators

"'That's what your people want—private eyes!'"

OTHER FROM BEYOND PRESS TITLES

Escalators to Hell: Shopping Mall Horrors is a collection of neo-gothic tales, nostalgic yarns, capitalist monstrosities, and one stop shopping gone very wrong (or a little too right!). Featuring 22 stories by established and new horror writers from around the world examining the dark side of malls. With Christi Nogle, J.A.W. McCarthy, Angla Liu, Jennifer Lee Rossman, Lor Gislason, and more.

Xanax Hamster is your new home for horror flash fiction trunk stories: horror shorties that have been rejected a lot but just needed to find the right home. Volume 1, issue 1 features stories by Sasha Brown, Die Booth, Timaeus Bloom, Tehnuka, Phillip E. High, Ryan Cole, D. Marmara, and Amelia Gorman. Each copy is hand-assembled in our basement, which is a lot of work so please buy a copy.

Frank London Brown was one of the most important voices in Black Chicago literature, whose 1959 book *Trumbull Park* is a vital portrait of segregation in the North. He died of leukemia in 1962 at the age of 34. Between November 1959 and November 1960, he wrote **This Is Life**, a series of very short stories for the *Chicago Defender*. This book collects all 133 stories for the first time.

frombeyondpress.com